The postman never brings anything to my grandmother. He passes in front our house shaking his head, then looks away, as if reduced to begging, we expected him to give us a letter. Anyway, my grandmother said that she does not want to see him stop near our house.

- No news, good news! We're good aren't we? We haven't even received a letter saying Happy New Year and good health or Happy Birthday Mother!

- So you say! Don't you want to receive a letter from France like Man Elisia? Her daughter writes to her.

- She writes to her! She writes to her! What do you know? Perhaps you know what's in the envelopes! Go fetch water by the spring instead of being a know-it-all!

My mother is smiling in a photo that my grandmother keeps in the white iron biscuit tin which was placed on a pile of neatly ironed sheets in her wardrobe. My mother's first name is Aurélie. Since my birth, I have lived with my grandmother, Ms. Julia Benjamin. We call her Man Julia or Man Ya. I know that my mother left for France on a big white ocean liner. Sometimes, Man Ya gets annoyed and shakes her head. Then the thoughts that are stirring behind the wrinkles on her forehead transform into bitter words. Immediately, I ask the good Lord to let me become a part of the colony of ants which are going hurriedly through the cracks of the floor boards.

- She doesn't know how to write! No. She never learned how to send a money order! How am I supposed to feed and clothe you? Maybe she is already dead over there in France...

We live in Haute-Terre, a small village in Guadeloupe, wedged between the sea and the mountains. Man Ya was born there 52 years ago. Me, I'm 10 years old. Man Ya works in the Sainte Marguerite banana shed. Every day, she gets up at 4am to go pick, wash and sort the bananas which she then packs into boxes which will leave via the ocean, just like my mother Aurélie. Man Ya and I live in a wooden two room house.

I only have my grandmother. She knows my character and tries her best every day to correct my quirks. Man Ya often says that she will always have enough strength to correct me if by chance I go down the wrong path. Of course she doesn't laugh every day, but we have good times together when she talks about her childhood, criticizes her old friends or applauds my recitations. However, she doesn't like to see me laugh too loudly. It seems that that brings unhappiness into the house. She yells:

- Stop making a scene in here fool!

Man Ya tells those who ask that my mother sends her a large money order every month to cover my expenses. She has taught me not to contradict her when she lies about this topic. She says:

-That way no-one will question you or pity you. They won't be saying all around that your mother has abandoned you. Do you understand? That's the reason why I invented the story about the money order...

Man Ya's face changed when she realized that the postman was happily and decidedly coming our way.

-Ms. Félicie Benjamin? Is that here?

-Yes, replied Man Ya simply, while taking the envelope which was bordered in blue, white and red that was addressed to me. She mumbled something between her teeth that I didn't understand and looked at me up and down as though I had made a mistake that was bigger than my head. She placed my letter on the kitchen table and pretended to ignore it for the rest of the morning. In fact, I sensed her distress as if a bothersome person had come to visit us. At some point, Man Ya sat in her rocking chair with her eyes closed and rocked nervously until she fell asleep for a nap. I tiptoed out of the gallery, taking care not to make the old floor creak. I hoped to be able to at least touch the letter which was desperately calling me from the kitchen table. I moved forward slowly but surely. I could already see the corner where the little blue plane landed when Man Ya suddenly awoke.

- Félicie! Where are you my child? ... Féfé!

She asked me to go and get the letter after lunch.

- Open it! We won't hide anymore. The river cannot wash away that which is destined to you. No-one escapes their destiny.

- Yes, Man Ya.

- Read everything that is written on the envelope and don't try to take advantage of my naïveté.

Man Ya doesn't know how to read. She doesn't take pride in it but is pleased to repeat that being able to decipher symbols on paper alone does not ensure intelligence nor does it automatically open the doors of reason. She settled herself comfortably in her rocking chair, put on her glasses and crossed her legs. I didn't need to look at her to know that she was rolling the corner of her apron between her fingers.

- It says: Ms.Félicie Benjamin. Route de l'Ermitage. Haute Terre. Guadeloupe.

Man Ya let out a sad sigh and urged me to continue with a hand signal.

La Cité, June 3rd

My dear daughter,

I already know that you will be shocked to hear from me after such a long silence. I could not do otherwise. After many difficult years, I now have a better life. Know that I have thought of you every day since my departure. I am sure that your grandmother is raising you well and loves you very much. But it is now time to join me in France where your family is waiting for you. I am married and you have a little brother who is 4 months old.

One of my friends will be in Guadeloupe during the vacation. You will return together. You can trust her.

My dear daughter, I hope that meeting me will make you happy.

Hugs and kisses.

Your mother Aurélie.

Every word pronounced made Man Ya's face become more wrinkled while her sighs transformed into groans. At the end, she cried:

- Your mother is tearing off my two arms and bleeding me to death...

She pulled me towards her, pressed me against her large breasts and hugged me for a long time.

That was the first time that I saw her in tears, and tears also started to roll down my cheeks. A bit later, when she got a grip on herself, she asked me if I wanted to live so far away from her. I responded that it would please me to know my mother.

- In addition, Man Ya, I can't refuse because she has already paid for the ticket and it costs a lot of money. Also, she says that she thinks of me every day...

- Ingrate! spit Man Ya.

That terrible description made me feel worse than a beating from a belt. And then she added:

- You're just like her huh! Same animal! Same fur! All you need are two or three honey covered words and you give her absolution. You forgot all of those years when she never even checked to see how you were doing! Go ahead! Go ahead! Run into her arms! Go and meet her! You don't see that she sees me as dog shit! Not a word for me. Do you think that's normal Félicie?

Whatever she was mumbling between her teeth got lost in the hubbub of her repeated nose blowing. We cried together until the evening.

The days passed. Long, long, long. It was necessary for me to seriously control my conversation topics in order to avoid slipping up and I had to eliminate certain painful words from my vocabulary like departure, plane, mother, letter, trip, go, leave, go... Man Ya was sweet with me, even in my absent-minded moments. She said:

- Enjoy your vacation, Féfé. Enjoy. You don't know what will happen tomorrow.

We lived, to all appearances, just like before the letter but my days dragged on while I waited. Waited without showing it. Waited for mommy's friend. Waited for something to happen to relieve the time spent trapped and waiting like the genie in the magic lamp. The entire month of July was dedicated to this infernal wait. Man Ya prayed fervently that the woman wouldn't find the way to Haute-Terre and that she would get lost for eternity in the neighbouring woods. She set out candles at church and kneeled for long periods of time at the feet of the patron Saint of Family. That afternoon, she woke up suddenly and searched for me in the bed while tapping the sheets blindly.

- Are you there Féfé? Come closer to me. Come and heat up my old bones.

-I'm here Man Ya. I'm just going to pee.

Then she went back to sleep with her arm wrapped around me tightly like a real karate grip. I found myself stuck with my nose nestled in her odorous armpit. We were Siamese sisters. Her breathing reverberated in me as well as each one of the stirs of her large rumbling stomach.

My best friend's name is Laurine. She is also our neighbour because we share the same courtyard. Her father, Robert, is the most famous fisherman in Haute Terre. People come from far away, even from Pointe-à-Pitre, to buy his fish. Man Justine, or Titi, Laurine's mother, always shows her teeth when she cracks a smile. Titi is sweeter than the coconut sorbet that she sells on Saturday afternoons in front of the municipal stadium. Titi never screams, she seems to hold back her voice which only knows how to whisper quietly in an eternal convalescence. Nothing like Max, Laurine's older brother. He has a voice like a foghorn in the form of a professional crab hunter who sees himself winning the Tour de Guadeloupe on bicycle.

Every morning, after my chores (dishes, sweeping, filling up of water buckets), Laurine calls me until Man Ya agrees to allow me to leave. Man Ya does not like to know that I am far away from her sight. She always has a thousand and one pieces of advice to give me before I can leave.

- Don't go to people's houses that you don't know. Don't play with boys who look under girls' dresses. Do you understand? Don't go far far where you can't hear my voice and so on and so forth.

It's like a popular song that plays on the radio every half hour. We remember the music but the words go through one ear and out the other. They fly away and get lost beyond the Savannah, in the big ears of the green hills inhabited by the spirits of some maroons. They say that after sundown, the maroons dance and sing zouk at a fast pace which competes with the drums of yesteryear. I love Man Ya with all my heart, but when she starts to ramble, I feel like whistling. To cut her litany short, I exclaimed:

- You said: Bad mother! Bad daughter! Not the plane, Jesus, not the plane!... Afterwards, you held my hand.

-Stop talking nonsense over there! You dreamed that.

-I'm not lying.

-Go, go, go and play Félicie. And come back before midday, if not!

Man Ya stood in the doorway. I felt her gaze on my back for a long time. Since the letter, she never stops watching me. She often caresses me, a bit mechanically, like when she smoothes her pleated Sunday dress. I think she still loves me even though she doesn't say it. She often calls me stupid, she-devil, insignificant. But her nights are filled with nightmares which make her tremble in her sleep. Man Ya is waiting for the woman who's supposed to take me from her.

In mid-august, seeing that mommy's friend hadn't come yet, Man Ya started to believe in the efficiency of her numerous prayers. Sometimes, I find her smiling sheepishly. Her little eyes sparkle. She says:

- The vacation is finished, sweetheart. No-one is coming to get you anymore - she laughs - I know your mother better than she knows herself. Not serious for a penny! You saw yourself in the plane already huh! Anyway, don't be sad, you don't know what was really waiting for you over there. Sit close to me and tell me one of your recitations.

I cried yesterday evening. In my head, I'd already taken the plane at least a thousand times. I had even imagined our reunion. Yes, my mother made a fool of me. Man Ya is already telling everyone that i'm not going to France anymore. She gives me little consolatory taps on the head in front of people and laughs quietly at my deception. She has lots of things for us two to do.

- You've grown a lot during the vacation, lovey. All of your dresses are too short. Come here for a bit let me take your measurements.

- Yes, Man Ya.

- You're lucky, you know. You'll meet back up with your school friends and stay in Haute Terre.

- Yes, Man Ya.

- Tell me what you were going to look for over there with your mother who was never interested in you? What would you have been able to do in France's cold weather? There are even people who die from the cold. You understand?

- My mother isn't dead!

- She isn't dead! She isn't dead! Enough insolence! Well, i'm telling you and you can go back and tell her if you meet her someday! Listen! For ten years she was dead and she came back to life just to poison our existence.

It was a prayer war. On Sunday, I prayed with all my might that the woman would come quickly.

She came when we least expected it. The idea of the trip left my mind bit by bit like one of those dreams which seems real while you're asleep but deflates miserably at sunrise. According to Man Ya, she had found her quiet serenity. The woman placed a brown suitcase in the middle of the kitchen. She smiled widely at everyone then kissed us like old acquaintances. Man Ya wiped her cheek with the back of her hand.

- Aurélie has told me so much about you?

- Oh, really? Told you what exactly? asked Man Ya with a puzzled look.

- She loves you a lot.

- Did you come to take Félicie?

- I'm not taking her today. We will leave next week. On Tuesday. I just came to bring the suitcase and give you the date of her departure.

Sharp words flew like arrows. The woman didn't let herself be intimidated by the old, crabby woman who was usually my sweet grandmother.

- Do you have the ticket here?

She had to see it to believe it, like Saint Thomas.

- No. It's at my mother's house in Pointe-à-Pitre. You can trust me. I'm an old friend of Aurélie's. We've known each other for... with her nose in the air, she appears to be counting their years of friendship... Yes, seven years!

-You're lucky! Man ya smiled. She had intercepted one of her adversary's little darts that she broke like a matchstick.

- That's a real privilege, we haven't heard from her in... ten years, well counted.

At this point, Man Ya got up. It was the signal to leave. She held out her hand, far in front of her to stop the goodbye kiss.

- Well, I won't hang about any longer. My brother is waiting for me in the car. He must be cooking in the sun.

- Mommy's friend had a small smile in her voice.

- Yup, goodbye! muttered Man Ya, who pushed the suitcase with the tips of her feet with a profound disgust twisting her face when the woman wasn't looking. She cursed quietly to express her anger but in reality she was in dismay. With this woman's visit in the flesh, my departure had suddenly become real, came alive, inhaled and grew just like a balloon in the little wooden kitchen. I didn't dare to speak anymore, say everyday words or even lift a finger to try. Fortunately, an already defeated Man Ya had gotten into the rocking chair. She let out an involuntary but loud sigh. Pffft! Miraculously, the balloon burst at the same time as well, pfft!

All week long, Man Ya put away my things and sewed late into the evening. "So that you'll be presentable and they won't say that you were walking around in old clothes in the streets of Haute-Terre", she said. She made me three beautiful dresses, two skirts and two blouses. She often chewed up the ends of her words that I didn't understand. At night, she couldn't sleep. Man Ya talked and talked and her words flowed like the waters of the Carambole River. Man Ya loves me.

Tuesday.

My suitcase has been ready since yesterday evening. I had already said goodbye to all my friends, especially Laurine, Max and their parents. Man Justine hugged me so tightly that I felt like a soldier who was going off to war.

Mommy's friend came to get me at 3pm. We will be leaving Guadeloupe at 8pm. This time, Man Ya didn't come close. She stayed in the courtyard, seated under a large mango tree. That morning, the timely rain made the courtyard a muddy, slippery surface which she used as a shield.

- Don't come closer Miss! Careful... you're going to slip in the mud and sully your pretty shoes. I'm coming, i'm coming.

She never came. The woman was in a hurry. The look that she gave me told me clearly that she understood Man Ya's game.

- Go ahead, go tell her goodbye Félicie. Kiss her for me. She was grieving but I couldn't do anything.

With a relaxed appearance, she ran her fingers, with her long red fingernails, through her short, straight but magnetically wavy hair. She was beautiful.

Man Ya shelled black eyed peas with her head down.

- I have to leave now, Man Ya. The woman is waiting for me. Goodbye.

I was a bit awkward. I stood up straight in front of her instead of throwing myself in her arms. All because I didn't want to cry.

Man Ya raised her head, looked me up and down then declared, in a prophetic tone:

- Go! I know that you'll be back. The woman is waiting on you, go. Forget your miserable life with me, but never forget the good manners that you learned here.

- Yes, Man Ya.

I kissed her with all my might. My lips were like suckers on her hot, humid cheeks.

I held back my tears until I got to the path that leads to the highway. The woman took my hand and pulled me a bit.

- Your suitcase is too heavy, Félicie. What did your grandmother put inside of it?

- My clothes Miss, and my books and some yams and sweet potatoes and a small breadfruit, I think.

- Your grandmother is an old fool. You'll be forced to leave all of that at my mother's house. And stop calling me Miss. My name is Marie-Claire.

- My grandmother isn't silly.

- Don't be angry Félicie. I was just kidding. Here, look, it's my brother's car. Ok good, we're headed to Pointe-à-Pitre.

From the time that the doors slammed, the car took off. Her brother drove quickly. The tires screeched and I felt like we were turning the corners at 200 km/Hr. I was forced to hold on to the seat tightly to keep my balance. We flew past the countryside in a blur. Instead of sitting quietly, Marie-Claire told her brother the story about the yams, sweet potatoes etc, that were in my suitcase. He put his head down on the steering wheel and laughed but his foot was still pressed down on the gas pedal. He laughed loud, like me. If Man Ya had heard him, she would have said: "Stop making a scene over there!"

When we arrived in Pointe-à-Pitre, Marie-Claire told the story about my suitcase again. Her whole family tapped their thighs, dying with laughter. It's the first time that I've been separated from Man Ya. With my eyes closed, I pictured her sitting in her rocking chair, rolling the corner of her apron between her fingers and mumbling to herself. I'm sure her spirit must be hanging around Raizet, around the planes at the airport.

- So are you happy to be meeting your mother, child? Marie-Claire's mother turns me around and asks me a bunch of questions. Are you happy to be taking a plane? Will you be scared? Do you want to go to France?

- I don't know miss.

-Here, have a slice of cake, I made it. Go ahead, eat it, it won't stay in your stomach, I'm telling you.

-Thanks, miss.

Since my arrival this afternoon, I've been sitting in the same place. My butt cheeks are stinging me. I'm in a hurry to leave this house. Supposedly Marie-Claire would be back soon but it seems to me like she left hours ago.

When she returned, she was frantic. She was buzzing like a mosquito. We need to hurry up. We are going to miss the plane. Oh my God! The suitcases, the bags, hurry! We will never get there on time. And then, all of sudden, she started to cry. Her mother hugged her and gently wiped her eyes.

- I can't believe that I am leaving so soon. This new separation is killing me, she says while sobbing.

Full of compassion, her mother started to caress her hair which Marie-Claire did not appreciate at all. She pushed her off fiercely.

- Stop, you are messing up my hair!

The beautiful woman stood in front of a big mirror and started to fix her hair. Then her smile came back:

- Let's go, Félicie! You need to wake up for a bit! Fix your hair and pull up your socks. We are leaving.

Everyone hugged each other one last time. Her brother stacked the luggage in the trunk of his car and we left. It was a terrible thing to imagine that I was approaching my destiny. I was starting to realize that my name was actually registered on the list of passengers. I had to board the plane. I was made to climb up those narrow open stairs, over there on the runway, like a big mouth which would swallow up humans on behalf of the enormous belly of the plane. I was like a sleepwalker, my body was walking towards the plane, but my spirit was far, far away. Marie-Claire was rushing in front of me. At the same time, she was turning around and shouting:

- What are you doing? Hurry up! We are the last ones!

She was moving like Father Murray's old horse. Before I knew it, I was seated and had on my seatbelt. In the plane, the air-hostesses, who were dressed in blue like police officers in Haute-Terre, were going back and forth between the seats. Their lips were of the same red as those of Marie-Claire, but they had white skin and blonde or light brown hair. Marie-Claire took out a newspaper and started to read. It was night. Man Ya had to have been asleep for a long time already. The plane slid gently on the runway before takeoff. I held onto the arms of my seat and closed my eyes. I felt that famous cake starting to come back up. I clenched my teeth and pressed my lips together. Suddenly, the plane lifted off the ground and raced into the clouds. Through the window, I saw a part of my country which was studded with lights like a sky full of stars. It was shrinking, shrinking.

After dinner, Marie-Claire made it clear to the air-hostess that I wasn't her daughter. Then, she asked her for some blankets and told me to go to sleep. I kept my eyes open for a long time in the dark. Sleeping in mid-air! Even birds don't do that! They look for some kind of branch where they'll perch their bodies. And I, who only knows how to walk on my two legs, was supposed to fall sleep and forget that the plane was flying over the Atlantic Ocean while going through the clouds. In any case, sleep wanted nothing to do with me. Thoughts were going through my head. I was trying to envision my mother's face. I was also imagining her husband, giving him a mustache, a nice smile and two strong arms to welcome me. I could even picture the baby, my little brother, in his blue and white crib, a drop of milk remaining on his chin. Last night, Man Ya removed a faded picture with crumbled edges from the biscuit tin where she keeps her important papers. This picture dates back ten years and I've seen it hundreds of times, especially in secret away from Man Ya. My mother is incredibly pretty...I believe, without being vain, that I resemble her a bit. Her face radiates the joy of life. She's holding a hat in her hand and her dress, blown by the wind, covers her slender thighs. "She was twenty years old at the time, commented my grandmother. I never saw her smile after that."

-Do you believe that she is still as beautiful?

- I don't know. Who knows. You'll have to ask her friend. You will be able to examine her quite closely when you're living with her. Go ahead Féfé, take the ointment from the drawer and come rub my legs for the last time.

- Yes, Man Ya.

- Tonight, tell me the truth...Do I, your grandmother, live a miserable life?

- Oh no! I have never been miserable with you...I do not every know what color misery is!

- You're a rascal, Féfé.

It's been five hours since we've been flying. Marie-Claire opened her eyes and started to read again.

- Is my mother beautiful?

- What?

- Nothing. Are we going to arrive soon?

- Yes, but you still have time to take a nap. Close your eyes and sleep!

- Yes, Ma'am.

- Well, go to sleep!

I closed my eyes because I could feel that her eyes were trained on me. Suddenly, it got colder in the plane. I pulled up the cover, peeped through one eye and saw that Marie-Claire who was doing a crossword puzzle in her newspaper. Outside the window, the sky was black.

2

When I cautiously put one foot then the other on France's soil, I wasn't any less excited than the first person on the moon. Marie-Claire gave me a little shove and I moved forward like a robot. In spite of the sweater that I put on before leaving the plane, coldness fell on me with the same ferocity of a hurricane that was jealous of the tranquility of a little Caribbean Island. People were hurrying all around me, with a sad clown face mask plastered all over their face. I waited to see more white people but at first glance, there didn't seem to be many more than in Guadeloupe. Marie-Claire seemed happy to be back. She walked through the crowd in a disinterested way with the confidence of someone who, after a long trip, was returning to their childhood street and recognized her friends' faces and sees her parents' home directly in front of her. She calmly left me in front of the phone booth, told me not to move and said she'd be back soon. I felt like everyone was watching me suspiciously, the way that citizens look at foreigners. I followed Marie-Claire with my eyes for as long as I could so that I could maintain my composure. I asked myself if she was capable of leaving me there just like that, like a forgotten suitcase. My throat was dry. That's what I was thinking about when she came back with a man. She was making hand gestures while talking when suddenly, she pointed her index finger in my direction.

- Your mother couldn't come because of the baby. Say hello, Félicie. This is your new daddy.

- Hello sir.

My new daddy! As though I had an old one and we were about to replace him. He was small for a man, dark like Man Ya, he didn't have much hair and no mustache like I'd imagined. He looked at me, bent down and kissed me on the cheek. His perfume rolled around my ears and entered my nostrils before zigzagging between the people who were waiting for their luggage. It wasn't a fragrance that came from a small bottle of cologne. It had a strong nutmeg odor mixed with a fresh coffee aroma from the lands which bordered the rivers. After a while, he put a hand on my shoulder before saying:

- We're all going to get along well, you'll see!

- Yes, sir.

- Call me: Papa Jo.

Will there come a day when the words Papa Jo can leave my mouth without these little stones which are rolling around now between the papa and the Jo?

Mommy's husband has a two tax-horsepower car that is the same model and color as that of the Father from Haute Terre. Sitting all alone in the back between the suitcases and the bags, I followed the passing façades with my eyes. Sitting wide-eyed behind the glass, I asked myself what I was doing there. Papa Jo and Marie-Claire had completely forgotten about me. Just as one feeds pieces of bread to a hungry dog who would never be full even if his master's hands were empty, Marie-Claire responded graciously to Papa Jo's pressing questions. He wanted to know everything about his beloved Guadeloupe:

- Five years, yes. It's been five years since ... it's not a joke. Is such as such place the same? Oh really, they've built a new city hall! A highway! You don't say: a highway! Who goes across this hill and this river where I used to go long ago to put my crayfish traps!

And then:

-Not true! Man Unetelle died last year! My ancestors, my ancestors, my ancestors! They closed the Richemasse factory! In spite of the many canes that were crushed there! And the distillery! ... it's bankrupt! ... And this, and that, and this place and that person. Every now and then, he took his eyes off the road and glanced at his informant as if to read the truth of her words on her face. Marie-Claire looked straight in front of her, sometimes letting a big smile escape, which was escorted out by the red, polished nails on her long hands which flapped like the wings of a bird that was taking off. Outside, everything was grey. People were hurrying about in the streets between the buildings and the cars were similar to ants on a construction site. They were going in each direction, innumerable.

Papa Jo stopped in front of a large mosaic, it was on one of the walls of the building where Marie-Claire lived.

- I'm not going up, Marie-Claire. Aurélie is waiting on her daughter.
Marie-Claire shot a quick glance at her luggage and Papa Jo got out of the car.
- I'll put them in front of the elevator for you. Will that be okay?

- You're afraid that you're going to get in trouble, said Marie-Claire while laughing on the pavement. White smoke left her mouth as she laughed.

-

Trouble! ... Who? Me! responded Papa Jo while looking at me but I had already lowered my eyes.

- Go on, give me a kiss, Félicie. We'll see each other soon, don't worry.
When she slammed the car door, bits of cold air came in and landed on my suitcase then slid down my neck like a snake. I shivered.

- It isn't much further away, said Papa Jo. You'll see, we'll make a beautiful family! You're nice, I hope. Because your mother has been waiting on you for so many years. She loves you a lot, you know.

- Yes, Papa Jo.

In my head, the “Papa Jos” sped by as quickly as the cars on a smooth road but as soon as they were supposed to pass the bridge where thoughts transformed into words, the little rocks filled my mouth again.

- That’s it, we’re here.

He parked opposite a big grey building, twin brother of a whole bunch of others that stood in front of a long road and parking lots.

- This one’s ours, 3. Put that number in your head, Félicie. 3.3.3. Staircase B.B.B. It’s easy, huh! Building 3, staircase B ...

I should have predicted that mommy lived on an apartment block. Those who spoke about France said that over there, people lived in chicken coops. Perhaps because of her letter where she spoke about her “better life," I had imagined a real house, like the ones pictured in the Maison Françaises magazines that Titi bought once or twice a year to give her decorating ideas. A real house with a fireplace, a tiled roof, flowers in the balcony and a little driveway lined with gravel.

- Hey, look up. The window pane with the madras curtains. Count from the first floor. He held my neck. You go up to 10. Good, now count five windows from the left. You see! ... that's our house! Are you happy?

I said yes because he seemed quite happy with himself.
- Yes, Papa Jo.

But on top of the building, in the clouds, Man Ya's face smiling face said:

- Weird house! That's life in France! Well, I prefer to stay in my old house with my two feet on the ground, rather than to go up to the sky in my lifetime.

In the entrance, there were rusty, dented letterboxes with doors that were halfway off, that were sitting there miserably like the old tongues of carnival masks. On the yellowing walls, painters had tried out their palettes, scribbling here or writing their phone numbers there.

- It's the kids who do that! explained Papa Jo while pushing me into the dark elevator.

He pushed the nasty button several times. Nothing happened. He waited, his eyes on the ceiling. He started again. He waited then he punched it.

- This elevator is a real piece of sh... I don't feel like taking ten flights of stairs with your suitcase on my back.

He laughed. Then suddenly, the elevator snorted then took off with an unpleasant noise. After a long pause — he smiled at me gently. I lowered my head. He was comforted by the infuriating noise; I was worried about the reason why the numbers 3, 6 and 7 weren't illuminated. Would this elevator obey Papa Jo and stop on the 10th floor? The doors opened with an incredible racket.

- Get out quickly, Félicie! Or you're going to be trapped.

My heart was beating quickly. The number 1035 jumped in front of my eyes. Papa Jo was searching for his key. Mommy was behind the door. I hardly had time to see her face but I was already in her arms, pressed against her chest, breathing in her milk odor. She threw herself on me just as a thirsty person falls on their knees with their mouth open in front of a clean water source. Then, holding me with outstretched arms, she looked at me from head to toe.

- You're big!

- Mommy, you look just like your photo!

- Oh really? What photo? Her voice had suddenly hardened. Oh! You forgot to put on your skates! Jo, you're overdoing it! You're killing me with housework! ... Speak softer or you'll wake Mimi. She gave me a little smile then went towards the kitchen, gliding silently on the black and white linoleum which shone like an immense enamel checkerboard. Papa Jo showed me the pile of clean skates behind the front door. For the first time in my life, I could practice living room skating.

Mommy's house is as quiet as an empty church. Exhibited are porcelain canopies which are lighting a big Formica dresser, a rectangular table framed by four chairs which are covered by bright red velvet and paintings of a still landscape with lush green plants lined up in the soil.

- He spoke softly, come see your room, Félicie. It's been ready for a year, with the floral bedspread and all. However, I'm warning you — he lifted a threatening finger — your mother doesn't like untidiness, uncleanliness, noise and such.

We barely heard an imperceptible snort but mommy had already thrown on her skates and made her way to the baby's room.

- That's it, you woke him!

- But no, Lili ...

- But yes, Jo!

Papa Jo took the baby in his arms and rocked him a bit then he held him out to me like a living gift.

- This is your little brother Michel... Are you afraid of babies?

- He is so tiny...

- Go ahead, take him! You have to get used to it! said mommy. Mimi, Mimi, Michounet! Look who's here. It's your big sister. It's Fé-li-cie! Michou, Mimi...
Mommy's eyes gleamed as she caressed Mimi and murmured sweet words to him. Did she show me that same love before leaving me ten years earlier? I had just reappeared in her life and she has shown me less attention than her precious Mimi who she's seen every day for four months.

After lunch, I was the one who gave Michel his bottle. Mommy sat next to me. She started to talk as though she was talking to herself... "I've been waiting on this moment for a long time. I can't believe that we're finally reunited after so many years. I couldn't take Félicie before. Everyone can understand that... But now we're reunited. Forever."

I've been living in la Cité for a week. Building 3, staircase B, door 1035. I'm finally breathing properly on the tenth floor, as long as I don't think about the height in relation to the ground or look out the window. Sometimes, I feel like i'm still in the plane, suspended between heaven and earth.

Phew. I started to call him "Papa Jo" without forcing myself. I spit out all of the little stones. I don't have anything to say: he is very nice. And Mimi, he is too. He's like a fallen angel, as mommy would say. Mommy... she's the opposite. Mommy isn't a straightforward person like Man Ya who knows how to differentiate between black and white and night and day. Sometimes, she is sweeter than Titi, Laurine's mother. She squeezes me against her and suffocates me, covering me in kisses. Other times it seems to me as though she is more nervous than a crab trapped in a barrel. She glides from one room to the other on her skates. I never hear her come in, only if I raise my head do I feel her cold eyes fixed on me. I don't worry about it much because she's the same way with Papa Jo. Mommy is moody. She goes from happy to sad in less than two minutes. It's better to shut up! That's what Papa Jo does. I think that works.

Yes, my new daddy is nice. He's the one who takes me around la Cité. From building 1 to building 10. It seems that they get worse after 7. There, there are thugs who rob old ladies, smoke drugs and play with knives amongst themselves.

- Never go over there alone, Félicie. Promise.

-Yes, Papa Jo.

When school started, he accompanied me on foot the first day. The second day, he said:

- Now you know your way. You can make it on your own. But don't go towards 7 and the others!

In la Cité, there's a store we call "The Arab's". Whenever mommy grabs her purse, I put on my coat. She's always missing something to finish her meal.

- Don't lag behind! Count your money, Félicie!

I enter the dark elevator. I press the grimy button. I hit it two or three times like Papa Jo. I go up and down like a pro. Whenever I go shopping, I keep ten or twenty cents. Mommy checks her change but she doesn't say anything. With that money, I buy stamps and I write to Man Ya. I don't say anything to mommy because every time I mention my grandmother's name or I talk about Guadeloupe, she shuts down like a house when a hurricane is approaching and glares at me for hours. Papa Jo pulled me aside one day and pretty much begged me to stopped talking about it so now it's my secret. Man Ya doesn't know how to read or write but I trust Laurine. Before I left, I explained the task to her: read the Bible, my letter and Saturday's France-Antilles, respond to my letters. Thanks to her, Man Ya knows that I'm doing well. I often see her in my dreams, sitting in her rocking chair, paying attention to Laurine's reading and readjusting her glasses which have the irritating tendency of sliding down to the tip of her nose.

I have friends at school. They are all perched, like me, in the high houses of la Cité. They are French, North African, West Indian and African. Their accents are mixed, and their colors too. I'm in fifth grade this year. The teacher, Mrs. Dupuis, makes the same speech every day:

- The level is weak, students. You are already at a disadvantage. You must work harder than the others or you'll never be anything in life. Next year, you're going to learn English even though French is still a mystery to some of you. What are we going to do with you?

While she shakes her head with her mouth open as though she's trying to unhook all of the powerlessness that gripped her blonde curls, some students gauge this mountain that she presents to them daily, at the height of which, legs crossed, the English boy says "*hello baby*!". Others, bored by the sermon, yawned at the "weak level," the "disadvantaged" and the impossible "work harder than others!". Others still, start to imagine what "we" would make of "them": sausage meat, blood sausage, toilet paper or simply send them back to their faraway countries where people have the same color.

My best friend's name is Mohamed Ben Doussan. He's 12 years old and the last in the class. He's lived in la Cité since his fifth birthday. Before that, he lived in a country where both men and women wore dresses, where French wasn't spoken and teachers didn't play with their blonde hair. Madame Dupuis repeats contritely that there's no hope for him, he can never catch up. Fortunately, her words barely graze Mohamed and continue on their way, similar to little sheep in a blue sky bathed in sunlight.

Every evening, mommy searches my bag (she read that in the parenting tips in a Maxi magazine), and then she inspects my books. Sometimes she seems worried and asks me if I understand. In reality, it's easy for me. In Guadeloupe, I only got lashes once because of school. The teacher told Man Ya that I was being chatty. School was serious for Man Ya. Every evening, I recited my lessons standing up. She didn't really understand but she didn't mess about and I didn't want to stammer. She liked the recitations most. She asked:

- Tell the story about the little animals in winter (The Ant & the Cricket)!

I started:

- The cricket sang all summer when he found himself dying of hunger... Then, he begged an ant for food. I cried for her during Verlaine's "Autumn Song"... "And i'm going with the bad wind which is carrying me, from that, from there, like a dead leaf". The "Prayer of a little black boy", by the poet Guy Tirolien, made her force a smile. When I recited:

- Lord I don't want to go to school anymore; make it so that I don't have to go anymore... You know that blacks have worked too much. Why must we learn more from books that teach us about things which aren't from here.

She looked at me and squinted as though I was proclaiming my deepest thoughts and desires... I ended my recital with "The ring around the world" by Paul Fort... "Then we could make a ring around the world, if everyone would just give a hand".

In December, I made mommy sign my report card. I was first in class. The teacher summoned mommy and told her to put me in another school outside of la Cité next year.

- The level is too low here, because of the foreigners.

Mommy retorted:

- Well, my daughter is a foreigner too. Last year, she was in a local school in the countryside that isn't even on the map of Guadeloupe.

The teacher opened her eyes widely:

- Understand that it's for her own good miss! The riffraff will affect her if you send her to the secondary school in la Cité. I want something better for Félicie. She put her hand on my shoulder. Believe me; I don't usually do this type of thing. You know, I've been teaching here for four years, in the fifth grade. I've seen a lot of kids pass through here... Well, this is the first time that I've met one with such a high level. Her hand weighed a ton on my shoulder. If you push her, she will make you proud. Félicie is an excellent student, the best! I wouldn't want to see her waste her chances. There are so few in the projects.

With this last comment, she moved her hand and looked at me for a while. I saw the pity in her eyes. I felt as miserable as a lamb condemned to the slaughter. Mommy smiled at me.

When we returned home, mommy kissed me on both cheeks and gave me 5 Euros. She beamed:
- Good Lord, I didn't think that you would surprise me like that, Félicie. Well! Your teacher thinks highly of you... I didn't think that I would have a daughter who would come first in class one day. I swear!

- It's Man Ya who...

- What! She doesn't even know how to read ABC. Don't start talking to me about her, eh! Suddenly she was angry.

- Yes, mommy.

- Go ahead, it's not important.

Her tone was calmer but her eyes were glistening as though her anger was going to flow over as tears.

- Continue to do well, eh!

That's when Papa Jo arrived. He hadn't even taken off his coat when mommy gave him the good news. "Hey, Jo! Félicie is first in her class! She's very proficient it seems!" Papa Jo congratulated me and he slipped me 10 Euros while mommy was making dinner.

It's Christmas. Papa Jo remained in the apartment to take care of Mimi. I went to Paris, France's capital, with mommy via subway for the first time. My ancestors! My ancestors! You shouldn't be afraid to walk underground... The subway is a big iron worm that crawls in every direction by cracking its old joints. "Direction: Barbès-Rochechouart" said mommy. I closed my eyes until she pulled me by the sleeve.

- Félicie! You're sleeping. We're here.

If Man Ya was there, she would have thought it was a Saturday morning in Pointe-à-Pitre, on a sidewalk on Frébault Street. Blacks! More than in la Cité. Women everywhere, West Indian and African. Do we, people of color, who are so different from the whites, have the right to shop anywhere other than Barbès-Rochechouart in the stores with the big TATI signs? Whenever mommy returned from shopping in Paris, she only put TATI bags with big blue letters spread across the pink and white background on the kitchen table. Nothing but those bags. TATI, those big letters ran vertically and horizontally across the grey storefronts. Just like in la Cité, we heard lots of different languages or a bit of French that was distorted by accents. The sales assistants didn't really care. One might say they were robots programmed by a single language, French money. You had to fight to get a sweater, a dress, a pair of tights. It was aggressive shopping in a way. Everyone wanted to get a full outfit with only 10 Euros in their pocket. I left my 15 Euros at home. Far away from mommy's sight, the idea of sending Man Ya a gift came to my mind. I cried a bit the day before while thinking about my grandmother. I went to sleep with that same sadness in my heart... That's why I dreamed about her, I think. I saw her, wide-eyed, lying in her bed. The house no longer had its sheet metal roof and Man Ya was staring fixedly at the white sky covered in grey dirty clouds like those in la Cité. She was wearing her Sunday dress. The one with the pleated front and the beautiful pink, orange and mauve flowers. She was speaking but I couldn't hear her. I was just above her, on a cloud. I listened carefully so that I could hear one or two words. When she recognized me, her eyes started to roll, her eyebrows went up and down and her eyelashes fluttered but my cloud slowly got further away from the house. I was angry. I screamed and thunder rolled. I cried and rain started to fall on Guadeloupe. My tears woke me up. My room was dark. I didn't hear a single sound. Not even Michel sucking on his thumb. I had a hard time getting back to sleep and that's when Mohamed Ben Doussan entered my thoughts. Perhaps because he had once told me that his grandmother lives with him. He was so lucky... Man Ya was so far away from me. How was she really doing with her newfound solitude? Why was she calling out to me in my dreams? Was she in danger? A hurricane! A hurricane must have torn off the old roof of her shaky house! No... I chased off those bad thoughts with the back of my hand. Hurricane season passed two months ago!

In the store for girls, mommy offered to get me two dresses. In fact, ever since I brought home my report card, she's been quite generous and kind. She's been really trying to keep calm.

- It's Christmas, Félicie! We spoil kids at Christmas! If you want something else, I'll see if I can pay for it.

We left the store with two dresses. I wasn't brave enough to ask for anything else. Mommy held my hand in hers in the subway on the way back. We were pressed against each other and covered in our big TATI bags but we were safe and sound. I closed my eyes and tried to pretend with all my might that I was holding Man Ya's rough hand.

Mommy bought oysters and a big turkey for Christmas night. She told me that it was the tradition here and that I should adapt to France's customs. No lie, that was the first time I'd seen a whole turkey. Man Ya had never seen one either. In Guadeloupe, we only really use the turkey wings. We can get them in all of the grocery shops. They're frozen, sometimes with big forgotten white feathers that remind us of their membership in the chicken family. In Guadeloupe, turkey is poor people's meat. We sell it for 2 or 3 Euros per kilo. Sometimes, in the grocery shop close to our house, Man Zizine is forced to separate the frozen wings by hitting them with an old hammer before throwing them in the tray of her scale. Bam, bam, bam! She wrote " Wings from India" on the big black board that she put in the verandah of her shop. We laughed a bit but we couldn't help but think about eating a rare meat from such a far country. My third grade teacher taught me that it wasn't false from a historic point of view since gallinaceous birds: quails, guinea fowls, turkeys etc, were originally from India. We no longer laughed at Man Zizine's spelling.

Mommy sang in the kitchen while Papa Jo and I decorated the Christmas tree with golden balls and sparkling fairy lights. When Mimi woke up, he started to pull off the balls. Papa Jo laughed. Michel was now ten months old. He started to walk but he couldn't speak yet. He touched everything! Especially the things in my room. Marie Claire arrived around 7 with a kilo of blood sausage and a red-haired white man. Marie-Claire's cheeks were covered in powder, her eyelids were blue and her mouth resembled a red, round apple. She had big gold earrings in her ears that kept moving. And, as usual, her hands were flapping about as she talked. One day, Man Ya told me that people who can't keep their hands quiet while their mouth is moving aren't any different from mosquitoes who buzz and fly all around us looking for a patch of skin where they could sting us. In other words, they are people who have nothing to do except bother others and chat uselessly. Of course mommy didn't miss her chance to tell Marie-Claire that I was first in class. Marie-Claire pulled me towards her and kissed me on the cheeks four times. Then, she fixed her hair and returned to the arms of the man who had accompanied her. We were all sitting in the living room with our thighs pressed together like good little children. Then, silence took over the room. After one or two minutes, mommy jumped up screaming "the turkey! the turkey!". Marie-Claire imitated her and they dashed into the kitchen. Papa Jo, who didn't know what to say to Marie-Claire's boyfriend, smiled kindly. Sometimes, he would open his mouth a bit. I hoped that something would come out but then he would close his mouth back and stretch it into a silent smile. Stifled laughter was coming from the kitchen, where mommy and her friend were. I didn't have anything else to do but to look directly in front of me while I drifted off in thought. How was Man Ya's Christmas going? Was she thinking about me? Did she receive my card? We had spent so many Christmases together without turkey, oysters or chocolate... but what Christmases they were! No snow or decorated tree with shiny balls... but we never sat around straight with our thighs together in a living room where silence as our only guest.

Christmas flowers swayed sweetly in front of my grandmother's house from the very beginning of December. Our neighbors Robert, Titi, Max and Laurine were all Man Ya's children. We spent every Christmas and Easter together like a real family. Sometimes Man Ya would say that Titi replaced the daughter that she had lost in France. And, if she fell ill, Robert would act like a son as he would stretch her out in the back of his 404 Peugeot pickup and drive her to the doctor. All year round, Robert would fatten up a pig for Christmas. I'd met ten of them. They were all named Paulo. Robert said that he knew a soldier in the army back in the day who was more greedy than one hundred piglets. He scarfed down four or five dishfuls of any meal. He ate everything, with no preferences. He could pop all of the buttons off his shirt by just breathing and the belt in his pants would disappear, suffocated by the mass of his stomach. Robert thought that the name Paulo brought luck to the pigs since the first Paulo was big and fat by the end of the year. On December 24th every year around 3am, he would take his cutlass and his knives and head off to chop up Paulo. In Guadeloupe, our tradition requires us to eat charred pork and peas and soft yams. We spend all day cooking. However, the party really begins when the drummers come with their drums on their backs, crowned with the glorious assurance that they were the authentic descendants of the maroons. We served them, with respect, with plates of peas, yams and pork and we put a bottle of rum near to them. Voices rose to the heavens after the first few beats of the drums and my heart filled up. Every year, I thought that the Good Lord was going to come down to earth, even if only to sing with the drummers of Haute Terre and sing "... I see, I see... the star of the shepherd, Joseph, my dear servant..." — "Christmas night was made to sing about the coming of Christ", said Man Ya. "But also to enjoy, to fill your belly with food and drink, to dance and forget the bad days".

Mommy brought a silver platter from the kitchen with little blood sausages. Marie-Claire was at her side telling a funny story. They laughed like partners in crime. Mommy didn't even hear her friend's padless heels which were pounding and piercing the waxed linoleum.

- It's very hot. Eat quickly! said Marie-Claire while letting herself fall into the armchair close to her beau, who was looking into an empty glass. It's from Belleville. It's nice, huh, Bernard!

- Very, he responded.

A bit later, we had dinner. Mommy brought out a white tablecloth, china plates, glasses decorated with little flowers and silverware. Mommy was very happy. One might say that Marie-Claire's happiness was rubbing off on her. When I asked why they didn't cook the oysters, she even got up from the table, hugged me and laughed in my hair, while Papa Jo explained that these mollusks are eaten raw. I couldn't swallow a single one. However, I ate lots of turkey with chestnuts and chocolate logs. I even drank some Champagne. Marie-Claire continued serving herself, and she started to laugh louder and louder and pinch Bernard's neck. He was covered in red marks. Papa Jo held mommy by the waist as though he wanted to invite her to dance. Mommy turned around quickly and planted a kiss on his lips. That was the first time that I saw them kiss. That surprised me.

Around 1am, mommy asked me if I preferred Christmas in France or in Guadeloupe. To make her happy, I told her that I preferred Christmas in France. She puffed herself up as though she was sure she had won one more victory over Man Ya. I went to my room. I saw little lights twinkling through the window from buildings far far way in another city. It reminded me of the Toussaint in Haute-Terre and its cemetery that was illuminated by thousands of lit candles that were placed on the graves.

3

Mommy recommenced work in January. It's a race every morning. Mimi lost his cheerfulness. Whenever we take him from his bed at 5am, he starts to scream. His caretaker, whose name is Mrs.Simonin, is Guyanese. In addition to her five children, she takes care of six other babies during the day. She lives in building 4, stair E, door 3005. When she opens the door to her apartment, piercing cries come at us from inside. I see that mommy pretends not to hear anything even though she argues with papa Jo if by chance he ever raises his voice. With her sweetest smile, she hands Mrs.Simonin a large bag filled with baby bottles, disposable diapers and tins of milk. The caretaker yawns and arranges her rollers which hang loosely around her unwashed face. Every morning, mommy repeats that he'll be well-behaved, and then turns her heels while letting out a big sigh, so that she would no longer see Mimi's grimaces behind his tears. Sometimes, I accompany her. I carry the bag. I go up to Mrs.Simonin's house with her. We leave the building on foot. She takes the train and I return home. I now have a key, like the other children in my class. Even those who have stay-at-home mothers and whose fathers are unemployed. Like Estelle, for example, who lives in building 7. Her mother hardly ever leaves their apartment. Single, with three children, she lives with three children and lives off of allowances and grants. Logically, Estelle shouldn't have a key hanging around her neck. Papa Jo told me that it's because her mother is slumped on the sofa all day watching television programs, especially American series and other series like Santa Barbara or Dallas. It would hurt her to miss half a second to open the door. Either way, Estelle does what she wants. She hangs around the corners of La Cité. Mommy told me that she's known her since she was in diapers. So cute, so blonde. But now, she was no longer respectable. My friend Mohamed told me that he had seen her exit the cellar of building 8 several times. And building 8, everyone knew — , except the parents, was the den of the hell-raisers in La Cité.

Mommy works in clothing. That's what she told me to say at school. In reality, she sits behind a machine from morning till night. She sews the sleeves onto shirts on the assembly line. I asked myself what one would call such a job: sleevist, sleever, sleeve sewer? Papa Jo works with motor vehicles. Every day, he returns home saying that the factory is going to be closed. They're pushing the older workers out, sending the Arabs back to their country, and putting robots everywhere. Robot, that's the only word that really makes him angry. For him, robots announce the apocalypse. That means: ruin, misery, famine, the end of the world. One time, to calm him down, mommy said:

- Don't worry... They cut the fabric with lasers now and I'm still there, behind my little machine with my little spool of thread... You'll see!

Papa Jo shrugged his shoulders then suggested:

- And what if we returned to Guadeloupe before the robots kick us out!

Mommy opened her eyes wide and exclaimed:

- Shut up! You don't know what you're saying anymore Joseph!

When she pronounces all of the letters of Papa Jo's first name, that means that he should stop talking immediately if he doesn't want to see her get terribly angry and give him the silent treatment. So, he adjusted his skates, got up and slid quietly into the kitchen like an old man, where he poured himself a cup of coffee.

Normally, after school, I go straight home. I'm alone from 5:20pm until 7pm. I turn on the television right away, even before taking off my coat. The apartment makes funny noises when I'm there alone. It scares me. This afternoon, I followed Mohamed to his house. He said to me:

- My grandmother made loukoum. (Turkish delight)

I asked:

- What are loukoum?

- Cakes. Here!

At that moment, a little greedy candle lit up in my head. I saw Man Ya again, making a big doukoun. Loukoum and doukoun, they make same sound, they rhyme, and they're related. I could no longer resist the temptation.

Mohamed pressed the doorbell until someone opened the door. A big woman in a gold evening dress and a headscarf on her head opened the door grumbling. She gave Mohamed little taps on his head who then slid under her arms and ran to the kitchen laughing.

- I'm going to send you to the chotts, you'll see!

- The shits, you mean!

- No! No! The real chotts, over there, in the middle of the Hoggar. And you can stop trying to deafen me with the doorbell.

- Come, Féli!

His grandmother blocked my entry.

- Good afternoon madam.

- Good afternoon to you. Your name is Féli?

- Hmm, my full name is Félicie... it's Mohamed who shortens my name.

- Do you like Loukoum? And makrout and baklava?

- Yes madam.

- Where did you taste them?

- Hmm... at Barbes-Rochechouart...

It was the only place that I knew outside of La Cité. I must have said the magic words because the arm which was blocking my entry dropped at once like a dead branch from a tree. She pushed me into the middle of the living room.

- Actually, Féli, we say loukoum for short. The real name is rahat-loukoum, which means: comfort of the throat...

My saliva ran down my throat like the syrup from a candy rock.

- Go, go, Féli! Mohamed will give some to you. I made a lot of them this morning.

She smiled at me and her metal teeth suddenly flashed in the middle of her wrinkled face.

Mohamed lived in the same type of apartment that I did. A living room, a dining room, a small kitchen and three bedrooms. Four of us lived in my apartment while ten of them were crammed into his: Mohamed's mother and father, their five children, his grandmother Fathia and his two maternal aunts. The kitchen overflowed almost into the living room. The rooms were filed with bunk beds, plastic closets with zippers, larges suitcases and old boxes. Occupied in the kitchen, Mohamed's mother wore an evening dress that was similar to his grandmother's, except that the embroidery was battered, colorless and unravelling from too much washing. She dipped and stirred a ladle in a big stew pot where pieces of meat, carrots and other vegetables were floating around in a thick, red sauce.

- It's couscous, Féli. Have you eaten it before?

- No... I could already see myself with my entire mouth covered in red sauce.

- It's not ready yet! said Mohamed's mother without turning.

- Here, have a loukoum!

A real delight. With every bite, a thin layer of sugar coated my lips and I kept licking them after each application to make the pleasure last. Mohamed laughed because I was closing my eyes.

I eat them every day. My grandmother is a pastry enthusiast. You've seen her size! And her teeth! Hardened! She always says that it's the last thing that ties her to her country and the day she forgets a recipe will be the day she dies.

In the living room, Mohamed showed me his father's pipe collection, displayed behind a glass case...

- That one's the kouka, with the amber beak. That one's the narghile, with the long pipe; you see, the smoke passes through this flask filled with perfumed water before arriving in your mouth. Look at this one with the engraved copper. My grandmother is the only one who can translate the inscriptions for you. She has only lived in La Cité for three years, you know. Just after my grandfather's death, she came here with my mother's two sisters, Aunt Raissa and Aunt Lalla. You saw them right? They're sleeping in the bedroom... They haven't found jobs or husbands... so they eat loukoum and makrouts with my grandmother all day and talk about the homeland.

It was still pretty at Mohamed's house. There were silver trays, big carpets rolled out on the linoleum, heavy curtains finished with long fringes. I looked around, as though in a museum, while my nostrils were teased by the rich smell of meat in sauce which floated around the apartment.

Mohamed doesn't remember his grandmother's country. She always has to tell him that it's his country too since he was born there and lived there until he was five. He responds that his country is called France.

- Your parents' ancestors were Tuaregs from the Hoggar desert who sometimes stopped at Tamanrasset, under the archways of the bazaar. They only passed through, walking along the ochre walls shaded by tamarix. They were proud. They ate buckwheat pancakes, kept water in sheep skin bottles, did food shopping in the desert, were superb riders on their azelraf camels... Go ahead! Go tell that to your french parents since this is your country.

When we left, I asked Mohamed what he knew about the Tuaregs. He told me that they moved around constantly in the desert, wore a veil, a tagelmust, because of the sand storms, and they weren't afraid of anyone. I wasn't jealous, but it was necessary for me to wave the bravery of my ancestors like a flag. Maybe so that I could be more respected by Mohamed. Perhaps he'd see me differently if he saw the shadows of the maroons from slavery behind me. I said:

- I also have ancestors who weren't afraid of anyone. It was during slavery. They revolted. They broke their chains. They fled into the woods. When they caught them, they beat them until they could only walk on their all-fours. And if they did it again, they cut off a leg, then the other. At night, they attacked the plantations to liberate their brothers. They won their freedom.

- Do you think of them often Féli? Mohamed's eyes were round with interest.

- No, not really.

- Sometimes I dream that I'm galloping in the desert on my camel. I'm the fastest of the Tuaregs. I'm going so quickly that I leave everyone behind me. From time to time, I look back and I see them getting smaller and smaller. At the end, I'm alone in the middle of the desert. All alone. And i've lost my way. Then grandma Fathia appears. But her teeth aren't metal, they're white, made of porcelain. In slow motion, she shows me a place far ahead and says:

- Brave rider, if you go in this direction, you will find the Goléa oasis town.

Then I take a coin out of my pocket, a dinar. I throw it at her. She doesn't even try to catch it. And the coin gets lost gently in the whirlwind of the yellow sand. Mohamed stopped talking abruptly so that he could plant his rotten teeth into the loukoum that he was looking at and playing with during his story.

- That's a nice dream. Me, sometimes I dream of my grandmother. She lives in an old wooden house at the end of a hill, you know. I've always lived near to her. I often have the impression that she comes to speak to me during my sleep. I write to her almost every week but I don't get a lot of letters back from her because she is "alfa-bête", that's her way of saying illiterate. Sometimes, I was late coming back from school. She would be waiting for me by the door and would say:

- Why are you lagging on the road, Félicie? Don't you know that you have lessons to learn? You want to become illiterate like me! If you continue like this, you won't know how to read ABC...

- My friend Laurine writes to me in her place and reads her my letters.

- Féli, do you think that i'll be going to Year 7?

- Of course, Mo.

During the second and third term, I was still first in class. The teacher appealed to mommy again. She asked her if she had already enrolled me in the Joliot-Curie high school. Mommy responded that that school was too far from La Cité and that either way, the neighbors had assured her that the school which was just nearby was not so bad since all of the kids who were going into Year 7 went there. Therefore, why should I be the exception? If I was first in Year 6 then there's no doubt that i'd also be first in Year 7. The teacher argued a bit then shrugged her shoulders and looked at me as if to say: I tried everything; I wash my hands of it.

- You'll see, Miss. You'll see...

And it's upon these words that the vacation started.

Mimi has been trying to speak since the beginning of July. It's hard for him. We barely understand what he's saying and repeating himself irritates him. As for me, my breasts are starting to bulge through my T-shirt. Papa Jo makes fun of me all the time because I close the door behind me whenever I have to undress. Mommy bought me a pink and white bra. She promised me another one for the start of the school year. I wash the one that I already have once per week. On Saturday, Marie- Claire came specially to do my African braids. I sat there from 2pm until 9pm. My back hurt for two days but it was worth it. I have sixty plaits with multicolored beads at the ends. My plaits go all the way down to the end of my back because Marie- Claire added fake hair. It's great! It was absolutely necessary for Man Ya to see me with my new hairstyle. So, with Mo and Mimi, I went to the Photo Booth in the mall, two kilometers away. I don't have the right to go so far. Mommy doesn't know anything. The people in La Cité aren't gossipy even though they see us pass every afternoon, Mo with Mimi on his back, me and my sixty African plaits. Mo knows lots of interesting places. He told me that one day, when the baby is bigger, we will all go to Paris. I've been responsible for Mimi since July 15th because his caretaker Mrs.Simonin went on vacation with her large family, as Mo calls it. Papa Jo will be working until July 30th and mommy until August 10th. I manage how I can. Mommy taught me how to light the stove and tells me every morning not to light the building on fire. I bathe him, feed him, we play, we read and we watch TV while we wait for Mohamed with whom we are going for a walk. The trips are our dessert. We prepare for them from morning. When Mimi hears the bell and sees Mo, he knows that we will soon be leaving so he starts to scream and jump for joy.

Mommy does not even suspect Mo's existence. She really thinks that Mimi and I spend the entire day in apartment 1035. When she returns, around 7pm, ten minutes before Papa Jo, she finds me in my room telling Mimi stories about prince charming, sleeping beauty and the child eating ogres. She kisses us and immediately sends me downstairs to buy bread, salt and a kilo of rice at the Arab's. At night, I never look her in the eyes because i'm ashamed. Once, I tried to tell Papa

Jo that I had a friend, Mo, and that he walked kilometers on afternoons with Mimi on his shoulders. At the last minute, I held my tongue.

Man Ya should have received the two photos that I sent her, one of me alone and the other of Mohamed with Mimi in his arms. I asked myself what she thought of Mo when she saw his yellowish complexion and black curls. She must have classed him as mixed (half Black, half Indian). In the photo, he was showing his large square teeth which were pierced by cavities. I told him to brush his teeth after eating loukoum but he couldn't care less. He says that they're ruined for good, that they're rotten and that later on, he will wear dentures. In spite of that, Mohamed is good-looking. I see him on his camel, with his head covered by a white tagelmust and his body enveloped in large, dark veils. He was carrying me. Sitting behind him like the passenger on a motorbike, I laid my head on his shoulders and put my two arms around his waist. We galloped through the Hoggar desert. And this voyage would be endless, far from the buildings of La Cité numbered 1-10. Maybe we can take Mimi with us, to save him from this vacation that we're spending between the television and the mall that we know by heart.

Sometimes, I think about Laurine and the awesome vacation she must be having in Haute-Terre. I daydream about the friends that I left over there. And my heart clenches. I imagine Laurine climbing the mango tree in the yard to bring back piles of round mangoes. I see her mouth stained with sweet, thick orange juice. I close my eyes tightly and pray that I wake up in Haute-Terre, at the foot of that same mango tree, after a nap in which my dreams had taken me to mommy's dull La Cité. I also remember the river baths that we took with all of the neighborhood kids. We combined our money to buy a large bottle of orange Fanta or Coca-Cola. After the bath, we took turns drinking it, holding the neck more greedily. During the vacation, Man Julia screamed that I would drive her crazy. She didn't like girls that followed boys around in all of their comings and goings. But, when I asked for her permission, she didn't know how to refuse. She was a bit like Madam Fathia. She always pretended to be upset. She promised me lashes and extraordinary beatings but her heart was warm and nice like the midday sun which dries the laundry laid out on the grass in front of the house in three minutes. It's strange, when I lived with her; I only heard the names that she called me like "stupid". Now that the sea separates us, other words come to mind. Yes, each one of her sentences ended with "mommy's dear little girl", my little darling or Féfé darling. Once, I called Mimi that, "my little darling". He stopped wriggling about and stared at me dumbstruck with his big black eyes. We don't speak Creole in the apartment. It isn't forbidden but it isn't welcome either.

The other day, I was telling Mo about the summers that I spent in Haute Terre, the sea and river baths, the games we played in the courtyard under the shade of the mango tree and the walks in the woods. Mohamed's eyes were less round at the mention of my maroon ancestors. He told me that he'd never been to the sea since his birth. Of course I laughed immediately because I thought it was obviously a joke. I figured that he obviously thought that I was naïve enough to believe such a thing. He swore on his grandmother Fathia (who he loves more than his mother) that it was the truth, in front of Mimi. Unbelievable but true! Mohamed thinks that he'll never see the sea. He has no money to go there! What's more, he knows lots of older kids in La Cité who have never touched the sea except by caressing the television screen where waves break like in a bowl. That's when I realized how lucky I was to have lived in Guadeloupe for ten years with its rivers and the sea where I could dive and the woods and hills to climb. Also, to have lived on the ground, in an old wooden house with grey boards and a rust covered roof, similar to Bernard's (Marie-Claire's fiancé) face. Guadeloupe is shaped like a butterfly but you mustn't believe the people who say that it is heaven on earth. Every year when hurricane season was approaching, I trembled with Man Ya in our shaky house. And, Soufrière, our terrible volcano, could also wake up suddenly and swallow us all. The ground could start to dance under our feet and then knock us over. It would be as though the butterfly were batting its wings for a desperate but impossible takeoff. However, there isn't a day that I don't think about my life over there. I want to go back, that's all I'm thinking about right now. I know that Papa Jo has that same wish, unlike mommy. If he is unlucky enough to bring it up, mommy changes her tone and calls him by his full name. Papa Jo stoops and shivers.

- Joseph! I've already told you not to bother me about that! Never!

When Mo comes over, he opens all the doors and sticks out his neck outside. He inevitably ends his visit with a surprised nod and says:

- It's always so prim and proper here.

Yesterday he came earlier with couscous. We set the kitchen table and we behaved like Mimi's parents. We talked and imitated the characters from the series Dallas.

- I prepared this couscous specially for your Bobby.

- Thanks Pam, dear. You're an excellent cook. Here, take this diamond that I bought for you in Paris on rue de la Paix. Yes, this morning I popped over on my private jet.

- Oh! Thanks Bobby, you're a sweetheart.

- It's nothing Pam. It's nothing at all. Just a little stone.

- Sue Helen would die of jealousy, the poor thing. I don't think JR has given her anything this week. She's going to make a scene then go and get drunk. Anyhow...would you like a bit more couscous, Bobby my love?

Mimi looked at us and laughed. All of a sudden, he frowned. His words were fighting to get out of his mouth. We trained our eyes on his lips. Finally, he cried:

- He's not Bobby. Mo! Mo! Mo!

We guffawed in the couscous. The grains fluttered around our plates. I said:

- What! What did you say? Repeat that! He pointed at Mo and repeated:

- Mo! Him, Mo! Not Bobby, Mo!

I had a dream.

It happened in la Cité in winter. It was the evening and I was sitting with Mo on a bench in front of building 8. It was snowing. Mommy was watching me through the window. Papa Jo was next to her holding Mimi in his arms and calling me to come in. I didn't move and neither did Mo. We were almost entirely covered in snow. In the distance, we heard Kassav's music. The song "Siyé bwa" was coming from one of the apartments in la Cité. I turned my head a bit towards building 7. A woman was approaching us from that direction. She was wearing stilettos and dragging her feet a bit because of the fairly high snow. I thought that she should have worn boots. She was carrying a little black glossy bag under her arm. Her white coat had a large sky blue collar. With her head lowered, she walked past us without even slowing down. Snow continued to cover us. Maybe we looked like two snowmen sitting on a bench. I closed my eyes for a moment. When I reopened them, the woman in the white coat with the sky blue collar was standing in front of me. It was Man Ya. That gave me a real blow to the heart. I jumped up. I shook off the snow that had hardened on my winter jacket and I ran towards her. Mo did the same.

- It's Man Julia, Mo! It's her, my grandmother!

Mo didn't seem to believe it. While dusting off his mouth that was covered by a thick layer of snow, he mumbled:

- You're dreaming, Féli! Wake up! How could she be here?

I didn't ask myself that many questions. She was there, that's all that mattered. I saw her, I touched her and her kisses melted the snow that covered my cheeks. Her words were sweet in her hot breath. After a while, she opened her bag and took out two keys. A golden key and the other silver. In the hollow of my ears, she whispered these obscure words:

- Here's what I came to bring you. With the golden key, you will liberate your friend from dark jails. The other will help you to open the door of knowledge. If you use them wisely, you will rip through the air above the sea and you will be in the yard under the mango tree again.

I don't know why but I looked up to the sky at that moment, just in time to see a gigantic butterfly flying over building 9. It disappeared into the clouds, batting its majestic wings. When I started looking for Man Ya,

Mo started to laugh , then he sat back down on the snow covered bench.

On August 1st, Papa Jo exclaimed:

- Thank you God, let the holidays begin! Then he put a shopping bag on the living room couch. All day, he hung around the apartment watching television shows that he wasn't interested in. After lunch, Mimi started to cry. That was bound to happen. Mimi had developed a taste for afternoon walks. As soon as he started to scream: Mo! Mo! Mo! I looked at him wide eyed. Papa Jo asked me several times if I understood this Mo! Mo! Mo!I said no! I felt the weight of my betrayal through the nasty look that Mimi was giving me, a real Massaï warrior arrow. Papa Jo took him in his arms and cuddled him until he fell asleep. Of course I had warned Mohamed about Papa Jo's presence. We were all disappointed, especially Mimi. Papa Jo would have understood the reason for our escapades but he didn't know how to keep his mouth shut. The proof? He told me a secret that mommy had been keeping for months. It was a surprise for me. I had to swear not to tell anyone. From August 15th, we would be spending ten days in the countryside with Marie-Claire and Bernard. Papa Jo was very excited. It's in Sarthe, Félicie! He took out a Michelin map and unfolded it in front of me. Look, look! Right here, that's the little village where we're going: Aubigné-Racan! Marie-Claire says that the people there are very friendly. It seems that we can buy milk, eggs and vegetables directly from the neighboring farms. Not far away there's even a river where we can bathe. I asked Papa Jo how we'd get there and he responded rather naturally that the old two-tax horsepower car would make it. For him, she is much tougher than the flashy cars being made by robots today. Replacing it wasn't even on his list of distant plans. He and mommy had been saving all of their money in an account so that they could buy a real house one day on the ground.

It's been a week since i've seen Mohamed. Thursday, after a shopping trip at the Arab's, I hurried over to building 5, staircase H, door 8002. He wasn't there. His grandmother Fathia told me that he was hanging out at the mall with his brother Rachid. I scribbled him a little note:

Mo, i'm leaving with my family on vacation on August 15th. I'll be back on the 25th. Thinking about you. Big hugs.

Your friend Féli.

The Aubigné Racan house is very old, with thick stone walls. Marie-Claire opened all of the windows and shook the curtains. Dust flew all around us. She laughed loudly, as usual. I like Bernard, her fiancé. He doesn't talk much but he's a sweet bread, as Man Ya would say. Marie-Claire calls him Pipou. He told me that his grandmother spent her youth in this house and it had never been modified since then. He never comes here during the winter because it is impossible to heat correctly.

The vacation passed quickly. Too quickly. We had fun. Mommy was less annoyed than in la Cité. In any case, Marie-Claire's laughter is contagious. Everyone was affected by it, even the farmers who sold us eggs and milk laugh in advance when they see her. The day before yesterday, she decided to milk a large cow. The farmer said that it wasn't necessary anymore since they had machines. She begged and pleaded so much that he handed her a bucket and an old white sheet. There were at least twenty of us there watching her do it. Her long red nails pulled bravely on the cow's udder, who continued to chew grass. Marie-Claire couldn't get one drop of milk from the huge breasts but it was great to see her play around like that, especially at her age. The farmer offered her a round of cider. I think it must've been a while since he'd laughed so hard, with tears in the corner of his eyes.

Ten days of vacation isn't much but you mustn't complain, it's better than nothing. Everyday we drank fresh milk, ate vegetables, fruits and fatty rillettes. We bathed in beautiful rivers and walked like real tourists through almost deserted villages, supported by canes and walked around the church square, greeting each other with a slow movement of the head.

The vacation is definitely over. We left Marie-Claire and Pipou at Aubigné Racan and we made our way back to our suburb. Papa Jo was right: the two tax horsepower rolled to the parking lot in la Cité like a marble without even coughing one time.

4

Tomorrow is the start of the school term. I haven't seen Mohamed once since my return.
The school is as ugly as Papa Jo's factory. Man Ya taught me never to be ashamed of being poor, but standing there in the schoolyard, shame covered me from head to toe. Frankly, I was happy knowing that she would never see me in this big box with dirty windows. There are paintings of bombs on the walls. There are messages, bizarre caricatures and pornographic drawings everywhere. The walls are frightening, nightmares even! Worse than the clinks of the stairs in the buildings of La Cité. There are war cries of hate and revolt and paintings of torture with big, twisted, multicolored letters through them. There isn't one round, yellow sun with happy rays or even a flower in full bloom.

At school, the big kids are terrifying. Some of the boys have a beard and a mustache and the girls resemble made up women. I noticed that the smaller new kids were a bit isolated and I joined them. I searched for Mohamed with my eyes until the bell rang.

High school really is a different world. Primary school was sweet as honey. Here, we tremble when we pass the gangs in the corridor. We lower our eyes and hope that they don't see us. I have five teachers. The French teacher also teaches history and geography. She introduced herself like this:

- My name is Ms. Bernichon. You are my first students. I CHOSE this profession. I hope that you will not make me regret it. Your school has an appalling reputation behind it. We will change it together. I am happy to help you should you require any assistance.

Light, sarcastic smiles floated across her lips. How could these newly arrived little kids of grade 7, dwarves among giants, even begin to imagine saving the reputation of a high school called “the Vault” from the beginning of time...? This teacher was extremely naive! We filled out our forms with the attitude of an unemployed man who was writing out his curriculum vitae for the thousandth time. I was about to write mommy’s profession when Mohamed arrived, escorted by a supervisor. Ms. Bernichon glanced at her list before appointing him the empty seat at the back of the class. When he passed close to me, he brushed my arm and smiled at me.

At the end of class, the students got up hurriedly as though someone had just shouted “ Fire firemen!” Then they ran down the corridors and hurtled down the stairs. I didn’t mingle with them. I hung around a bit to put away my things, hoping that my friendship with Mo hadn’t expired with the summer. When I raised my head, I saw him about to step out of the classroom door.

- Did you have a good vacation?

- Yeah.

I didn't want to show my joy in seeing him too much. That disturbed me. He wasn't comfortable either. I asked:

- And your grandmother, does your grandmother still make loukoum?

- Of course! When are you coming over to eat some?

He smiled with all of his rotten teeth.

We rejoined the others and sat next to each other in science class. He told me that he had thought about Mimi and I but that he had found new friends. I wanted to know who they were; he said I didn't know them.

At midday, I hoped that we would go to the canteen together but he had other things to do. We separated in the schoolyard. I could see that he was pulling away. He had grown up. His jeans reached his ankles like Michael Jackson's pants. His brother Rachid's old fake leather jacket weighed down his shoulders like the weight of a miserable destiny.

Marie-Claire and Bernard are going to be married in the month of December. Marie- Claire's parents are making the trip specially for the occasion. The future Mrs. is telling mommy and Papa Jo about it very enthusiastically. Mommy will be her witness. They hug and cry, tapping each other's backs warmly. Papa Jo promised Pipou lots of coffee with milk before bringing out the bottles of wine. I had gone into my room when they started laughing while talking in veiled terms about the famous honeymoon night. I didn't feel like celebrating. Nothing made me laugh these days anyway. I don't understand Mohamed anymore since we've been in high school and that bothers me. He doesn't come to class often. His exercise books are dirty, he doesn't have any textbooks. If I want to talk to him, I have to run after him. And when I ask him why he's never there, he talks to me about his notorious friends that I don't know. He also says that it makes no sense showing up to school because he doesn't understand half of what the teachers are saying. Everything is so difficult for him. I think that's what turns him off. Me, I'm comfortable in maths and French. No problem... The other day, I scored 16/20 for my composition. She even read it to the students. I was a bit annoyed because I talked about going to Guadeloupe. Mo gave me a strange look as though I had lied to him. I talked about sea and river baths, picnics, walks in the woods. I described Man Ya in her old house, with the big mango tree in the middle of the yard. At the end, the class stayed silent, hanging on to my memories. After class, Ms. Bernichon called me. She said:

- I know all about Guadeloupe, you know. It looks like a big butterfly, right?

I shook my head.

Were you really over there during the summer holidays?

I said no.

- Were you born here?

Her eye was more powerful than a ray from a laser.

- No miss, I've only been living in La Cité for a year.

- Your heart stayed over there, close to your grandmother?

- Yes, miss.

- You know what? I have a plan – it's nothing official yet!

- I have a plan for a class trip to the seaside at Easter. I'm waiting for a response; I have the permission of certain people. The dossier will be complete in December. We'll see...

- That'll be great!

I almost cried. Of course I thought about Mo, who had never seen the sea. It would be as though, after spending many years wandering in the Hoggar and Sahara deserts, a proud Tuareg finally arrived at the edge of the beach on his Azelraf camel. He would remove his tagelmust and his caftan theatrically; he would throw them with a wide swing and dive fearlessly into the highest waves. Maybe if Mo went to the sea, he would find his way back to school.

When Marie-Claire and Pipou left, I went to kiss Mimi in his little bed. It was my way of asking him to forgive me. He was sleeping already. This afternoon, he saw a boy who looked like Mo on television and right away he pointed at the screen and started to shout "Mo! Mo! Mo!" Once again, I had to pretend as though I didn't understand what he was saying while Papa Jo tried to get him to explain. Poor Mimi.

On Saturday afternoon, we went to the mall as a family. It was November. It had already started to get really cold. Mommy sat Michel in the trolley and we inspected all of the shelves for two and a half hours. Sometimes mommy stopped for a long time in front of the piles of canned food. She would take one, turn it around several times, and then put it back sullenly. She would take up another one, an identical one; throw it into the cart then put that one back also. Papa Jo looked at her without saying anything. He was happy to push the cart, stop and start again behind mommy who was walking in front of us like a tourist in a museum. As for Mimi, he only had one idea in his head; grab the multicolored cans and the cellophane wrapped packages. I looked at the 501 jeans on the clothing shelf. Mo loves them so much, they cost 60 Euros. Mommy assured me that we'd find the same ones at TATI for 9 Euros each.

I saw Mo in the parking lot with a group of big kids from building 8. He had his two hands in his pockets and his brother Rachid was smoking a cigarette and screwing up his eyes. Mo looked at me without seeing me. I had become identical to all of the other people who were arriving at and leaving the mall. Luckily, Mo was sleeping on my shoulder. I think that he would have gone crazy if he had seen his idol in flesh and bone. His friend who had vanished. It made me feel a bit of shock to see Mo with those boys because he didn't hang out with them at all before the summer vacation. I concluded that those were his new friends.

On Monday morning, I passed him a note in French class:

- If you don't come to class regularly, you'll never be able to go to the sea!

I looked away when the message arrived in his hands. At the end of class, Mo was waiting for me by the door.

- What's this story about the sea?

I responded:

- Have I ever lied to you before?

- No...

I changed the subject.

- What were you doing with those boys from building 8? You never liked them!

- They're cool. First off, Rachid takes me everywhere with him now... I'm the youngest in the group!

I jumped:

- You're part of that group Mo! They smoke, steal, drink beer and fight. It seems that they even have knives and attack old ladies...

- I'm not a baby anymore, Féli.

We walked for a bit at the same pace without saying a word. Then Mo asked me again where and how he could get to the sea. As I didn't have many details since Ms. Bernichon had spoken to me very vaguely about the seaside trip, I responded:

- Where? Does it matter? There is only one sea. Salted. It belongs to everyone. We don't care about the borders that men construct.

As I spoke, Mo's eyes grew rounder. I thought he was going to cry.

- When are we going to the sea Féli?

- Easter.

My self-confidence pinned him to the spot. Did I speak too quickly? If Ms. Bernichon's plan failed, he would be extremely disappointed. The hallway stretched out over my shoulder. I screamed:

- Math class!

We ran hand in hand. When we arrived, the teacher smiled like a tiger in front of his dinner.

- So love birds, you were hanging around in the hallway... Is Félicie giving special classes to 7 F's invisible man named sir Mohamed Ben Doussan?

The students snickered foolishly as though they hadn't heard a better joke in at least six months. When they calmed down, the teacher gave a pop quiz. It was easy for me but I already knew that Mo wouldn't do anything worthwhile. He looked at me desperately as though he was about to lose his ticket to the sea. I gave him an encouraging smile. I was too far away to help him. Like a beggar in the streets, he tugged Alpha's sleeve to get an answer. Sadly, if Mo was the weakest in class, Alpha was the second last. They were in the same boat.

Marie- Claire and Bernard got married. Mommy wore a light beige dress with a big lace collar and black high heel shoes. Marie-Claire's parents arrived in a Boeing 747. One would have thought that it was a group of tourists coming on a package tour. Thanks to them, the wedding hall was transformed into an extraordinary exotic garden where the beauty of the large tropical flowers: porcelain roses, lilies, anthuriums and lavender flowers, rivaled against each other. The blacks, who were more numerous, were leading the dance. Bernard's parents, who were a handful, seemed to be thinking about the last survivors of a decimated family. They had fun nonetheless, especially after drinking a few ti-punches and having their tongues burned by spicy bloody sausage. We partied until 4am. Around two o'clock, mommy and Marie- Claire danced together like two sisters who were shown no interest by the other dance partners. Papa Jo invited me several times. I wanted to teach him how to rap but he much preferred the zouk of Kassav or the violins of Malavoi. I would have wanted Mo to be there. He's a super dancer! At the end, I sat in a chair. I was half asleep but thoughts were still circulating in my head. The golden key was to be used to liberate Mo from prison and the silver key to access knowledge. Would Mo really go to jail? Behind bars, grey walls and barbed wire! I shivered. How would I liberate him? Where was the golden key hidden? I opened my eyes. Marie- Claire and Bernard were rocking slowly, holding on to each other without really following the music. They were alone in the world and didn't care that we were looking at them. Seeing them like this, I thought that they supported each other like two friends should all the time, one encouraging the other who is weak. I would have liked to support Mo that way.

Marie-Claire gave us an entire tier of her wedding cake. The next morning, while mommy slept, I asked Papa Jo if I could take a slice to a classmate. He said yes without asking any questions and reminded me not to be late. He yawned a bit then sank back onto the couch, facing the television. I quietly closed the door and ran down the hallway. Of course the elevator had broken down.

I hurtled down the stairs. It was cold downstairs. The wind pushed me spitefully as if to stop me from meeting Mo. I was struggling. When I arrived at building 5 on foot, I looked like the reed from Mr. De la Fontaine's "The Oak and the Reed". I braved through it. I wasn't afraid. The gusts of wind unleashed my braids and the multicolored beads and their ends slapped me in the face. I felt big and strong. I felt like I could defeat this concrete mountain where all of the people of the earth lived on top of each other. I had the entire world in front of me as well as all of its races. And Mohamed was somewhere around, behind this terrible grey facade, in these heights where the sea's waves would never roll, where the sand of the Hoggar desert, locked away like a useless hourglass, would never flow but through grandma Fathia's memories. To give myself courage, I thought about the maroons, the brave men that they couldn't enslave. I told myself that during those times, they didn't laugh every day, they didn't dance to zouk and they didn't eat wedding cake. When I finally arrived at Mo's door, I was reinvigorated. I told myself that like me, Mo was young. I was sure that one day he would leave La Cité to go and live by the seaside, sit next to the beach for long hours and watch the waves unfold, wind up and retreat. One day, he will no longer be a part of the gang.

Grandma Fathia smiled at me in her green djellaba embroidered with gold and said: Good morning Féli. The real friend is the one that's there in times of trial. She's a bit like Man Ya. She knows little phrases that have big meanings.

- Where is Mohamed, madam Fathia?

- Gone, always gone!

- I have a cake for him!

- Gone!

She made a big gesture with her hand to show me that in her mind, we couldn't hold him or catch him.

- Do you want makrout? I made baklava too...

Madam Fathia went into the kitchen prancing about and brought me back those eastern pastries that I didn't know how to resist.

- Do you like them?

- I love them!

- And do you eat couscous?

That's how grandma Fathia is, always ready to offer goodies.

- Yes, I eat them. But I don't have the time... Tell Mohamed that I absolutely need to see him.

- Yes, yes.

On Sunday, I figured that Mohamed and Rachid were close to building 8 with their gang seeing that the mall was closed. I wasn't wrong. He was really there. With those boys with the eyes that were sadder than the stairwells of the buildings of La Cité. Mo resembled Saint-Exupéry's fox, lost among the inhabitants of a planet where the sun, the water and laughter didn't exist. Me, I wasn't The Little Prince, of course, but a princess who had come to tame the fox and offer him my friendship; to offer him the golden key of friendship... the golden key from my dream! Mo, caught red-handed, had just enough time to remove the cigarette from his mouth before hiding it behind his back. I said indifferently:

-Mohamed, your grandmother says that there's a package waiting for you at home. It's urgent!

The big boys looked at him strangely. I winked at him and he followed me rolling his shoulders and hopping each step, the way his brother Rachid does. On the way, I asked him:

- Do you smoke now?

He was annoyed straight away:

- What does that information do for you?

I continued:

- I'm your friend, Mo. You already have cavities... your lungs will be as black as pieces of coal!

- I don't care!

- Not me, Mo. You're going to die before ever going to see the sea.

- You talk! I'll never see the sea. You told me nonsense.

- I never lie about serious things.

- When are we going then?

- At Easter! I swear. But if you don't come to school, your name will not be on the list of students. Mo, believe me! I'll teach you how to swim, to dive and float on your back.

- What's floating on your back?

- It's floating on the water like an old branch... you don't move a finger, you forget your body and you look at the sun. You let yourself be carried by the current. If you want, I can teach you how to stay underwater for three minutes without breathing. How to open your eyes underwater and swim like a catfish. I'll teach you how to roll in the sand, then how to bury yourself up to your ears, how to find crabs who are digging underground under the beach.

Mo looked at me without seeing me. His eyes reflected a sea covered with froth and a turquoise blue sky, like the ones we see on cartoons. His spirit had leapt over the wall of the grey buildings of La Cité and was sitting by the seaside. I held his hand to bring him back to reality.

- Ok Féli, I'll go to school... His voice was deep, as though it was coming from a cave.

- I'll help you to understand the lessons better. But I'm begging you, please stop smoking! We start doing it stupidly and bit by bit we become a slave to the cigarette... You've seen the boys of building 8! They smoke and they cough. They are all pale. Some say that they even take drugs that make you crazy.

- I've never seen them smoke anything other than Gauloises and Marlboro.

- You're blind, my word. Furthermore, they're sad. You're starting to become just like them, sad.

- We laugh sometimes...

- Go ahead, tell me about it!

- The other day, at the mall, Ken, who has the eagle tattooed on his arm, stole a CD...

- Then what!

Well, the security guard surprised him and ran after him.

- Then what!

- Well, Ken swung the CD right at his face. The guy found himself on his butt. The whole group ran away. We laughed after when Ken imitated the security guard who was running with the gun in his hand, like a fake cop from the Hawaii State Police.

- You find that funny? Mo lowered his eyes.

- You aren't my grandmother Féli. Stop with the speeches.

I was fussing but it made me mad to see him hanging about with the gang from building 8, like a fox cub from the sands who is wandering around the desert and waiting on the rest of the camp of Tuaregs.

The New Year came, all white. Everything is clean in La Cité. The sky had thrown a long, immaculate blanket over the grey streets. I looked out the window and I tried to imagine myself: a little black head behind a little pane among hundreds of identical others in a big, dark facade. I laughed at myself out loud. Mommy said that I was crazy to laugh for no reason, but papa Jo smiled.

Laurine sent me a parcel on behalf of Man Ya. It's my most beautiful Christmas gift even though mommy spoiled me, by offering me a Barbie doll. In Guadeloupe, I ran around behind marbles, or even after a kite that was escaping far away, with Laurine and Max. Sometimes, we spent minutes with our noses in the air examining the sky, before seeing the kite like a little dot in the blue sky. Mommy told me that French girls loved Barbie dolls, it was the ultimate gift. Anyway, in my package, which smelled like Guadeloupe, there was: a vial of castor oil, a white lace dress (hand sewn by Man Julia), an envelope containing a golden chain with a pendant shaped like the map of Guadeloupe, and in a page of France-Antilles newspaper, two vanilla pods, a stick of cinnamon and three nutmegs. I gave them to mommy, who didn't even say thank you. I don't know what she did with them. Maybe everything went down the garbage-chute. I asked myself if she's going to stay mad at Man Ya for the rest of her life. If I at least knew the reason for their falling out ... Unfortunately, I was never told a word. It's as though they stay on either side of the street, each one cloistered away in their house with the condemned windows and doors. Some say silence is golden but I think they should have chosen speech, which is silver, so that they could become mother and daughter again. One day I asked Papa Jo if he knew the reason for their disagreement. He hurriedly put his finger on his lips and I saw the panic in his eyes. If he kept it to himself, the secret had to be terrible...

I'll be going back to school in two days. I thought about Mo and the teacher who promised me a seaside trip through the entire vacation. They're now inseparable in my head. One can't function without the other.

The snow fell again this evening. I put on the gold chain and I fell asleep with the little pendant of Guadeloupe, which resembled a butterfly with its beautiful wings spread, in my fist.

Silence entered the classroom like an inspector on tour when she started to talk. Even those who would normally make negative comments out loud, the stupid laugh specialists, the lovebirds and their sweet words were silent. Stupefied. All of them. After the words: Seaside trip, Mo immediately looked at me. His eyed wide like the marbles planted in Mimi's stuffed bear. I felt proud of myself. Like a super girl. But we hadn't even regained control of our emotions when she mentioned the destination. Guadeloupe! I thought I was going to faint! I even thought about a heart attack, i'd seen that on an episode of Rick Hunter. It was a boy who had been given bad news. All of a sudden, his face turned white, words no longer came out of his mouth and his fingernails sank into the wood of his desk.

Mohamed's eyes were on me again but I didn't turn my head in his direction. I barely noticed the worried eyes of the students because a thick fog enveloped me. It wasn't until Ms.Bernichon called my name: Félicie Benjamin, that I fell back into the current dimension.

- Félicie Benjamin, you're from the country. You can introduce us to the country. You others, you're going to form groups to prepare exposés about this beautiful french Caribbean island.

The questions were pouring. How are we going to pay for the plane tickets? How long are we going to stay there? Where are we going to sleep? And what if our parents say no? But it wasn't the question of money that worried me the most. Fortunately, pocket money was the only thing that parents were required to provide. In fact, the town council, assisted by the departmental Council and several other organizations, had taken care of everything so that no-one would be excluded. It was the first time that a class from the La Cité high school was going on a school trip to one of the French Overseas Territories. The overjoyed students couldn't stop congratulating each other. The chatting took place under the watchful eye of Ms.Bernichon, who had planted so much happiness in our hearts.

That evening, I announced the incredible news at the dinner table. Papa Jo started clapping straight away while mommy stuffed a piece of meat in her mouth. She took her sweet time to chew and swallow before saying:

- Why are you so happy? And what if I don't send you?

Papa Jo let out a sigh and murmured a pleading "Lili". I stared at mommy without lowering my eyes. It was the first time that I had confronted her in that way. She held out for a bit then she turned away. I had won.

- You've changed, Félicie. A year ago you would never have acted so insolently. You're becoming a bad seed. Even the way you speak is different. You've lost your good manners.

I continued to watch her ferociously without responding. My eyes were stinging. Papa Jo gave me a smack on my knee under the table and I lowered my head, but only for him. At the end of dinner, I left the table without asking for permission. I put my plate in the sink and I walked to my room with my head held high and took big steps like an outraged queen. I put on my nightgown and dove under the covers. Before closing my eyes, I caught a glimpse of the Barbie doll with her legs crossed like a secretary on my shelf. She was smiling. I was so annoyed that I sprang out of bed and grabbed the doll and threw it into the shoe corner, behind my wardrobe. I went back to bed satisfied and I turned off the light. I held the little golden pendant that Man Ya had sent me in my hand. I wanted to go far, far away. Suddenly, in my head, the piece of jewelry which represented my country transformed into a real butterfly. A huge butterfly. Its wings flapping impatiently, ready for a fantastic flight. It was stationed in front of building 5. Mo and I got on. Mo was like a real cowboy. All of the people in La Cité were at their windows, open-mouthed, with their index fingers pointed at our butterfly. Old people who were looking without seeing for a long time yelled:

- A butterfly! A giant butterfly in la Cité! Come, come everybody! He's going to fly away with the children!

Actually, he carried us above the building which, from the sky, really wasn't bigger than Mimi's playing cubes. From above, we saw the cars as they filed along the highway. They were all going to Paris, leaving behind a black smoke like octopus ink. Mo held the reins. He ordered:

- To the sea!

I lay my head on his shoulders. My braids fluttered about with pleasure. The butterfly was going so quickly. Soon after, emerald green plains appeared. Then, we flew over mountains that were a hundred times higher than the buildings of La Cité. Big brown masses. Finally, the roar of the waves rumbled in our ears. Below, the sea, in all its majesty replaced the solid ground. Flying fish leapt into the waves next to a three-master which rolled out its numerous sails: the brigantine, the skysail, the mizzen topsail and also the big sail, the jib and the forestaysail flapped in the strong wind. But the most extraordinary thing was the transparency, the magical clearness of the water. And all of the fish of the Caribbean Sea, the underwater welcome committee, came to meet us. They flapped their fins in a profusion of colors. I recognized all of them, named them for

Mohamed: there, old grey ones; here, red snappers and blue and green catfish, look! The big rusty mouths, the Portuguese fish with the yellow striped stomachs; here, honeycomb cowfish in their hard bluish carapaces; oh! The leopard whip-ray with their big flexible tails like a whip. Mo was dazzled. The butterfly greeted them by batting its wings majestically. So, we had seen...

I didn't hear her enter, but her hand on my cheek interrupted my daydream. I opened my eyes and mommy smiled at me, resentful and sulky, I turned my head to the wall. Her hand was caressing my hair and it felt good. I wanted to continue sulking indefinitely so that her fingers would run through my hair until sleep took over again and put me back on the butterfly's back, in the middle of the clouds.

- Félicie, I have to talk to you.

- ...

- I know that I haven't been an exemplary mother to you. We don't know each other very well. In fact, we have never really talked...

- Why don't you want to send me to Guadeloupe? Are you afraid that I will see Man Ya again?

- Man Julia! Oh la la!

It was the first time that she said her mother's name in front of me. I turned around at that moment and I saw tears running down her cheeks, zigzagging like little water snakes.

Twelve years ago, your grandmother was very strict, inflexible and stubborn... I thought that she was stopping me from going out, out of spite. When I met your father, through some people, I accepted his invitation to the Haute Terre ball. She didn't want to give me her permission so I snuck out while she was sleeping. I danced until morning in the arms of my admirer. When I returned, she was waiting for me, sitting in her rocking chair. She rocked slowly, her face somber. I gave her the same look you were giving me today at the table. That's when we stopped talking. I came and went. Free, I thought. When you were born, shame seized me and I left. She loved you. I put the sea between you two and myself. I wanted to forget the past, redo my life. But you know that the past always catches up with us. I've thought about you every moment since I set foot in France. I saw you grow up, in my dreams. When I met Jo and he asked me to marry him, I wanted you to be a part of my happiness as well. But I didn't dare. It was Michel's birth and Marie-Claire who made me take the plunge... now the only thing left for me to do is to see my mother again, to patch things up.

- You'll let me go on the class trip, right?

She looked at me like a student who didn't understand anything about decimal fractions. I was touched to see her there, sitting at the edge of my bed, talking about her past and telling me about the father I had never known. I wanted to cover her in kisses and beg her to do the same with Man Ya, tell her that I'd found a father in Papa Jo, scream to her that speech was silver only because friendship was forged in gold. Silence, according to her, was only good for lifting the cardboard boxes that we were supposed to light on fire. Thank you Man Ya for having given me, in a dream, the silver key to access knowledge.

- Why don't you write her a letter? - I'll see, Félicie, I'll see.

5

Mo was a different boy with his hair cut and his face freshly washed. I almost didn't recognize him and that made me laugh inside. He was wearing a new pair of jeans, a black 501 t-shirt and big purple and white sneakers which were impeccably laced like military boots. A green shoulder bag was tugging down his left shoulder and a big plastic bag hung from his right hand. He seemed proud in spite of his rotten teeth. Together, we joined the overexcited children who were making a circle around Ms. Bernichon.

We sat next to each other on the plane but we hardly talked to each other during the voyage. Everyone was lost in their thoughts. I think he that he still couldn't believe that after this trip, he would have been to the sea. As for me, I was excited about the idea of seeing my country again; the streets of Haute-Terre, but most of all, my good old Man Ya. After the meal, we slept because time spent sleeping always brings a dream closer.

- Will we see that Guadeloupe is shaped like a butterfly when we arrive?

- No Mo. Soon we'll be up overhead. You will see the beach, the mangrove, the green hills, maybe the banana and sugar cane plantations and then the red roofs of the houses.

- When I was leaving, grandma Fathia told me : Travel, you will get better.

- She knows nice phrases.

- Will we be there soon?

- In about two hours.

- What will it be like for you to be back Féli?

- I don't know. I hope that Man Ya doesn't have a heart attack when she sees me. I didn't tell her because I wanted to surprise her. I regret doing that...

One by one my thoughts went to Man Ya, just like leaves blown by a strong breeze. Had she changed? And her health? Especially her old legs...I hadn't massaged them in two years. And Haute-Terre my beloved village where the midday sun beats down on the backs of children returning from school; where wandering dogs run around in packs; where cars and ducks travel along the winding asphalt roads. I closed my eyes to remember, get my bearings. From time to time, the voice of the hostess emerged from the loudspeakers in French and English, sweeter that the honey sprinkled baklava made by Miss Fathia's expert hand. When we came out of the clouds, Mo's mouth was stretched in a smile while he stared intensely under the airplane's wing. The white relentless waves came and went without stopping, splashed, withdrew and subsided in turns.

- The sea! It's the sea Féli!

Thursday afternoon, we left Ms.Bernichon a note that said:

"We must go see my grandmother in Haute-Terre" then we left.

Signed Félicie Ben Jamin

and Mohamed Ben Doussan.

I wrote Ben Jamin deliberately. Mo told me that would bring us closer together. It was as though our ancestors were cousins: the Ben Doussans and the Ben Jamins (Mo pronounces it Ben Jamine).

One week of swimming lessons and afternoon excursions was about to come to an end. The sea recognized Mo as one of its children. She took him in her arms, cradled him, carried him and patted him with her caressing wavelets. It only took Mo three days to learn how to swim. Of course I was happy but I did not share his blissful ecstasy. I had known these beaches since my birth. I had run on the sand thousands of times and dived into the sea. I vaguely felt like my place was somewhere else, far away from these children from sun starved projects. I studied, I ate, laughed and swam with them but my spirit left them the moment I breathed in my country's air again. Every day I heard nagging calls similar to the whispers one hears around the banana plantation: " Haute-Terre! Haute-Terre!"

whispered the deep voices. “Man Ya! Man Ya! Man Ya!” breathed the velvet voices. Haute-Terre! Haute-Terre! Man Ya! Man Ya! But Ms.Bernichon always put off the stopover in Haute-Terre until the next day. It seemed that all of Guadeloupe was to be explored, except Haute-Terre. Today's, Carbet Falls, tomorrow la Soufrière, the day after, the Mamelle mountains or the heart of Bouillante... and the museums, the beaches... I ran out of patience. “ Haute- Terre! Haute-Terre!” whispered the pushy voices. “Man Ya! Man Ya! Man Ya!” cried the other voices. Mo didn’t want to let me leave alone. We were in Pointe-à-Pitre. I saw the bus station in the distance. The multi colored buses waited and called by blowing the horn. The radios played zouk loudly. I recognized one of the bus drivers from Haute-Terre. His vehicle had hardly changed. The tiger paint on the metal was flaking a bit and one of the rusty, dented fenders of the bus was exposed in the sun. We found ourselves stuck between a fat Indian woman and a young woman who had a baby in her arms. “Haute-Terre! Haute-Terre!” the voices shout to the driver. The bus starts, backfires and lets out a cloud of smoke.

- Are there still maroons in Haute-Terre Féli?

- I don’t know. When I lived there, there was an old negro slave who was at least 90 years old. Whenever Man Ya saw him, she would say: “ He’s a maroon”. He would always repeat “ I’m a maroon! I’m a maroon!”. He lived alone in the woods just like the maroons of yesteryear and took care of his food garden. He rarely came down to the market. He only came to buy a bit of oil for his lamp, salt, oil, pigtails and a slice of salted cod. He was a part of the war in France in 1914. After that he returned to the country a changed man, saying that men on earth were more savage than the most ferocious beasts in the African jungle. A jungle that he hadn't even been to. He said he preferred to live alone in the woods from then on, away from human beings. It was his way of revolting. Sometimes when I saw him pass, so old, so wrinkled, a bit sagged, skin close to his bones, with his rusty cutlass on his shoulder, I thought that he must surely see the ghosts of the last maroons up there in the hills.

I saw Laurine first. In the yard, our yard. She was sitting, nose in the air, on the same bench where I used to sit. Feeling my presence, she glanced at us distractedly, before returning to her celestial contemplation. Then, just like in the cartoons when Tom realizes that he's about to pass Jerry without eating him, Laurine realized that her old friend was not 7000km away, but there, in flesh and bones, two steps away from her. Her mouth rounded in a stunned, silent O, and instead of running towards me like a sensible person, she ran in the other direction screaming Man Ya's name. I automatically turned my head towards Man Ya's house. She was there, in the doorway, like a magical apparition. When the sweet nickname left her mouth, I shivered like I would on a winter day and two tears moistened my cheeks.

- Féfé! My Féfé! How did you get here? Oh baby!

I kissed her. Her cheek was soft. Mo introduced himself giving her one of those kisses that he gives to Ms.Fathia.

- We came with our class, Man. Ya.

- I've seen the sea! declared Mo, as though an injustice had finally been righted.

- Poor thing! said Man Ya, while caressing his hair.

- I have a letter from mommy for you. She might come here next year with Papa Jo and Mimi, my little brother.

- Your mother! exclaimed Man Ya. Are you sure? When she left ten years ago, she swore that she was turning her back on Guadeloupe forever, that she was going to the country of the good people... What do you know, it's strange that I dreamt about her during the harvest moon last month... Go, go ahead, read me what it says.

Her voice was trembling.

My very dear mother,

Don't be shocked to receive this little letter after these years of silence. Youth is a bit like the first cousin of madness, you know. At twenty years old, we dream about our lives and dismiss the experiences of our elders. I was proud. I told myself that I knew more than you since I could read and write French. I thought that you wanted to stop me from living. Know that these years of silence amassed between us, high like a bushy hill deserted by men and birds, weigh on me as much as you. It's thanks to our Félicie that I have realized that speech is worth more than any form of silence.

Kisses from Jo and Michel. Your daughter loves you,

Aurélie

If Laurine hadn't come back with her mother, I don't think that anything could have torn us from the joyous state of bliss that transfixed us in the middle of the yard, a smile floating on our lips.

We followed Max and Laurine's steps to the beach after lunch:- catfish in stock with yams and Madeira wine that Mo had devoured after he was served like a prince by Man Ya. It was a nice afternoon. We ran behind crabs, got almonds from the almond tree by the seaside and swam. We swam towards the sail boats that were cruising offshore. At 5pm, Laurine's father returned from fishing. In the bottom of his small boat called the Concorde, red, green and blue fish flopped about in their final moments of life. Around 6pm, the sky suddenly got dark. I almost forgot that night comes so early on this side of the world. However, nothing could pull Mo from the magic of the waves. I had to beg him to join me. He still wanted to look at the illuminated liners that were on the horizon. He wanted to feel the lukewarm sea water covering his skin. To be honest, we completely forgot that we had run away. We weren't thinking about Ms.Bernichon or our classmates. We were like two young animals taken from captivity that found themselves back in their natural habitat and were acting instinctively on their newfound freedom.

When we returned, it was nighttime and Man Ya was a bit worried.

- Féfé! You shouldn't stay out so late! You want the zombies to take you?

A nice cow foot soup was waiting for us. I felt like I was living a dream. After dinner, we fell asleep naturally in the big bed on both sides of Man Ya, with our heads buried in her odorous armpits. By the way, she hadn't asked about the length of our stay, as though time and its string of hours were no longer important to her. I breathed in a swig of her odor with every breath. An expert mix of Marseille soap, cologne, sweat and old age created a new scent more intoxicating than the enormous joy I felt being back in this old rusty wrought iron bed. This bed that shared my dreams and nightmares and sighed with Man Ya because of some flu that she was chasing away by concocting secret teas.

Yes, more than that, this perfume which lies dormant in the hollows of the bed, represented my childhood in Guadeloupe.

In the morning, Mo ran to the beach with Max, Laurine's brother. His shirt fluttered around on his back like Zorro's cape. Max was in front of Mo pushing a patched air tube ahead of him. I didn't leave the house that morning. Man Ya and I talked about our two years of separation. I told her about La Cité and she told me about the events that spiced up the lives of the people of Haute Terre during my absence. We had so much to talk about that it was midday before we knew it. When Mo arrived, just in time to put his feet under the table and devour his lunch, he was already thinking about going to track land crabs with Max. I proposed a trip to the river but he rejected my idea with the back of his hand.

- Oh no! Not today! We have to go after the crabs... that makes money, you know. Max sells them by the roadside... it gives him pocket money.

I was jealous of Max but I didn't want to steal Mo's joy so I smiled and said:

- Get some for us too! Man Ya will prepare them on Sunday.

- Ok! Ok!... In fact, when is she making the doukoun?

Ms. Bernichon turned up on Palm Sunday. I had occasionally thought about this moment. I imagined that it would come. I imagined that she would arrive somberly, escorted by four police officers in khaki shorts and a mouth full of threats and blame. But no, she was alone, getting off of a bus. She was sun-tanned, wearing a pink tank top, a short white culotte skirt, pink espadrilles and black glasses. She walked calmly like someone who was certain that their steps would take them to the right place. Her blonde hair had become more voluminous and framed her face well. She looked a bit like my Barbie doll, which I had left sitting on my bed to smile at Mimi if he entered my room.

It was morning, 9am sharp. Mo had already dashed off to the beach trailing Max, always looking for crabs. Max was definitely a professional but the competition was becoming more and more tough. From seven or eight years old, the boys started feverishly making rat traps to catch land crabs, or even sinking down to their navels into the muddy water of the mangrove swamp, tracking crabs. The elders, of course, had vast experience and a solid know-how. They skimmed the beaches. As for Max, he only chased land crabs with yellow shells, sometimes striated with pink; they were chefs' preference. He kept them in an old barrel. He talked to them like pets and gave them green bananas, stale bread or leftovers. Once a day, he chose five or six crabs according to their size, attached them to a string and stood by the roadside. The crabs didn't last long by the roadside. The motorists braked hard when they saw the animals with the big claws. The tires screeched while the crab lovers took out their bills but it was Max who chose the buyers. In fact, it was difficult for him to let go of the crabs, but it was necessary. He didn't want them to fall into the wrong hands, even though he knew they would probably end up in a casserole. Ten Euros for six. One day, he'll buy a real racing bike which he'll ride around every day. When he talked about his future bike, he lit up instantly. In his eyes, the bike sparkled like the chrome on a Rolls Royce. However, he was giving himself the means to make his passion a reality and to perhaps achieve his dream one day .

- And you, Mohamed, what's your passion?

Mo, whose horizons were barred by the buildings of La Cité, knew what passion was the moment he saw the sea through the window of the Boeing 747... "The sea, Max. The sea is my passion".

- How will you make it over there in France?

- I don't know. Maybe i'll become a lifeguard. I think that they're schools for that over there. You know, my grandmother always told me that my ancestors lived in the Hoggar desert, that the sand was their kingdom. They were called Tuaregs. They're still some left. They spend their time coming and going in the desert without ever finding their way to the sea. Does that seem strange to you, Max?

- Are they crabs in the desert?

- I don't know. My grandmother only says that the desert is the biggest colonizer in the world, one which we could never fend off. The gale breathes on the sand and the desert advances. He takes villages one after the other and chases away their inhabitants. Maybe one day the entire world won't be anything but a giant desert...

- The Good Lord wouldn't want that, Mohamed. Hey! One question, do you think that we could find crabs in the desert?

- I don't really know. Maybe. There'd be a lot. Millions, billions.

- Yeah. In one day, I would have gathered enough money to buy my champion bike...

- You'd get lost in the desert, Max. My grandmother said that it is so big that one can go on camelback for days before crossing paths with someone else. She says that a man alone in the Hoggar is a dead man who believed that he saw a thousand oases in a ray of sunlight.

- Are you going to stay here, Mo?

- We came with our class and our french teacher. We ran away because Féli didn't want to wait any longer to see her grandmother.

Ms. Bernichon was listening to Man Ya's wise words and didn't hear them arrive in the yard. Mo was walking lop-sided, arched under the weight of a bag of crabs. A smile crossed my face. I was like a mother watching her son with pride and discovering how much he had grown up. That same morning, Man Ya asked why he spent all of his time outside, half of it in the sea, the other half following Max in the pursuit of white crabs. In a few days, he had become darker than me because he walked around shirtless from morning to night. Didn't he want to sit with us for a bit under the mango tree in the yard where we were resting? Man Ya didn't realize that Mo didn't have a minute to waste. He had three weeks, and not a minute more, to take advantage of Guadeloupe. Mo tensed as soon as he saw her. He didn't know that Ms.Bernichon, after a long discussion with Man Ya, had decided to let us spend this last week in Haute-Terre. Straight away, he said:

- You came to get us? Ms.Bernichon smiled.

- You ran away didn't you? Even though it was for a good reason, it wasn't nice to behave in that way. Luckily, everyone knows Man Benjamin here. Félicie, it's her country, I understand that! But you, Mohamed Ben Doussan, the knight, in shining armor you're going to go back with me, now!

With his head lowered, Mo gazed with interest from his toes to his fingers stained with mud, while his index, quick like a worm, sank into his ear to get the water out. When he looked at her in the silent yard, Ms.Bernichon saw the folly of her request.

- Well, you don't seem to agree. Ok, I'll leave you with Benjamin Félicie.
She got up.

- I have to return to your classmates. I'll be back for you on Tuesday morning. Don't forget that we're leaving on Wednesday...

She hugged us and left, her blond hair flapping on her shoulders. Mo watched her disappear like the dinar in his dream that was swallowed by the whirlwind of sand with his mouth open.

There were no beribboned bells, no chocolate chickens, no sugar-coated or meticulously painted eggs like in the mall in La Cité. Only crabs. Everywhere. By the roadside, in the markets, in the barrels. People prepared them with calaloo, others with white rice or curry, with dumplings, breadfruit... But everyone ate them. The pot covers hid big bites and legs to be sucked at length with your eyes closed. Man Ya is a calaloo specialist. We prefer to eat crabs by the seaside. The beaches are taken by storm. It's difficult to find someplace to put the enormous stewpots, roll out the tarps, spread out the mat, lay out the long chairs and put the grandmothers in the shade. Robert and Titi, Max and Laurine's parents, did what was necessary. We were close to the row boats, under a beautiful almond tree open like a parasol. After playing hungry in the water all morning, we enjoyed the calaloo. Mo, who had never even tasted crab, asked for more greedily. That didn't shock me. He devours anything that comes out of Man Ya's pot hungrily. He misses grandma Fathia's loukoum just a bit though. As for me, I couldn't eat one more bite so I left the rice on my plate. Laurine's father rubbed his stomach and said to me:

- Let the stomach burst, but don't waste the food.

After lunch, Mo, who couldn't sit still, proposed a walk on the beach. Full, Max snored on a mat. Mo, even though bloated by two dishfuls of calaloo, refused to waste his time on a nap. I thought a bit of walking would make digestion easier so I followed him. There was a beautiful ambiance. Here, men played dominoes while gesticulating and talking loudly while women babbled and gathered the dirty dishes. At that moment, others started to help themselves to some pilaf with enormous tongs that looked like robot arms in a compact heap of rice. On one hand, the children whose noses were in the air were amazed by a kite while others bathed and yelled.

- Let's go, Féli!

- And what about digestion? With everything we ate, we're going to sink to the bottom...

- No! We're going to stay on the shore, scaredy-cat!

- Ok! Ok! You'll have my death on your conscience, and, if the teacher goes to jail...

- Ok, come!

His entire body disappeared in a wave. I asked myself if that's what a great love was. An irresistible call... Yes, Mo had fallen madly in love with the sea. A real love at first sight. He needed to dive, swim, leap and jump on waves, disappear on the right to emerge suddenly on the left in turns with flying fish, cat, conger eel, dolphin and shark. I joined him of course... That's how the afternoon went. Little by little, the families left. Some of them put away their tarpaulins which had given them shade all day. Others piled their pots into the car. Mothers called their children who were playing in the sand. I saw one pick up her son and pretend to throw him to the sky. They both laughed. A vision of mommy with Mimi in her arms suddenly entered my head... my heart shivered.

When we returned from our baths, Man Ya was waiting for us with her famous doukoun with coconut jam. After three or four bites, and with his mouth full, Mo declared that his grandmother's loukoum had nothing on this thick, heavy cake. I took three more bites.

We spent five days at the beach, swimming and eating fish and five nights sleeping on either side of Man Ya like two nestlings under their mother's wings. Then Ms.Bernichon came to look for us. Mohamed and I promised not to cry but our eyes, filled with water, sparkled immensely. Man Ya was calm. The morning of our departure, I rubbed her legs for a long time with greenish, slimy ointment that came out of the half empty tube like a snake. She played about with my hair with her fingers.

- You'll be back soon to see your old Man Ya, Féfé... you're leaving again but in fact, I understand that you never left this house where we spent your first years. I saw you by my side every day, or on the road, coming to meet me. I heard your beautiful recitations. And every night, I felt your hot little body in the bed. All of my dreams were about you.

That's why my heart didn't give out when I saw you the other day at the end of the street. It's true, Féfé! You never left...

- When I was over there, I thought about you a lot, Man Ya.

- I have all of your letters here, in my old tinplate box, and your photos too. You're my sun, Féfé... That's why I'm no longer afraid about the kilometers that are going to separate us, you see. Nothing stops the sun from shining onto the earth, not even the passing of time, men's misery and wars...

When I told Mo these words, he told me that Man Ya and his grandmother Fathia had the same wisdom. And, I don't know why but my heart was less heavy when I said goodbye...

Ms. Bernichon told us about all of the trips and excursions we missed on the flight back to France. The rocks engraved by the Arawaks at Trois-Rivières, the Edgar Clerc museum that contained the Caribbean's relics and treasures, climbing La Soufrière... But I think she knew that we didn't care and that we had no regrets. Our week spent between the beaches of Haute-Terre and at Man Ya's house was worth more than a thousand tourist trails. At the end of the film "The spy who came in from the cold", Mo told me:

- You know Féli... I have a passion... like Max. His dream is to participate in a cycling race around Guadeloupe and become a grand champion. That's why he catches, feeds and sells crab; to buy himself a bicycle that costs at least a million dollars! My passion...is the sea. I think that I'm going to try to become a lifeguard, Féli. I want to teach others to love the sea. When I saw it the first time, my heart beat strong, loudly... Do you think I can become a lifeguard, Féli?

- I think that you are well on your way, Mo. - Do you have a passion. Féli?
- Yeah, it's a secret.

- Come on, I won't tell anyone...

- Meh! It's not really a passion, you know. I write. I write everything that comes to me... I have a book for that.

- Do you talk about me?

-Yeah!

- You're great, Féli.

Mo woke me from my sleep a bit before the landing. I had fallen asleep with my Guadeloupe pendant in my hand, my golden butterfly. The Orly airport had either weary or overexcited travelers. Ms. Bernichon counted and recounted her students. And then, standing at the end of the hallway were mommy and Papa Jo, with Mimi on his shoulders, eyes wide open and his mouth cracking a smile... My little brother Michel was overjoyed... My Mimi shouted... "Mo! Mo! Mo!" like a man who claimed to have lived among the Martians but was never believed. There was a real liberation in his cries, the assurance that he wasn't a figment of his imagination. Mo! Mo! Mo! That's the day when mommy and Papa Jo finally understood the famous Mo that had left them awfully perplexed so many times. As for us two, betrayed by Mo, we looked at each other like two thieves caught with their hand in the bag and we burst out laughing.

Made in the USA
Middletown, DE
03 May 2022